T0278759

DISPATCHES FROM PARTS UNKNOWN

DISPATCHES FROM PARTS UNKNOWN

BRYAN BLISS

GREENWILLOW BOOKS
An Imprint of HarperCollins*Publishers*

This book is a work of fiction. References to real people, events, establishments, organizations, or locales are intended only to provide a sense of authenticity, and are used to advance the fictional narrative. All other characters, and all incidents and dialogue, are drawn from the author's imagination and are not to be construed as real.

Dispatches from Parts Unknown
 Printed in the United States of America. For information address HarperCollins Children's Books, a division of HarperCollins Publishers, 195 Broadway, New York, NY 10007.

epicreads.com

The text of this book is set in 11-point Bell MT Std.
Book design by Paul Zakris

Library of Congress Cataloging-in-Publication Data

Names: Bliss, Bryan, author.
Title: Dispatches from parts unknown / by Bryan Bliss.
Description: First edtion. |
New York : Greenwillow Books, an Imprint of HarperCollins Publishers, 2024. |
Audience: Ages 13 up. | Audience: Grades 10-12. |
Summary: "Ever since her father died three years ago, Julie has had a professional wrestler run a constant commentary on her life that only she can hear"— Provided by publisher.
Identifiers: LCCN 2023053988 (print) | LCCN 2023053989 (ebook) |
ISBN 9780062962270 (hardcover) | ISBN 9780062962294 (ebook)
Subjects: CYAC: Grief—Fiction. | Wrestlers—Fiction. | Family life—Fiction. |
Interpersonal relations—Fiction. | LCGFT: Novels.
Classification: LCC PZ7.1.B63 Di 2024 (print) |
LCC PZ7.1.B63 (ebook) | DDC [Fic]—dc23
LC record available at https://lccn.loc.gov/2023053988
LC ebook record available at https://lccn.loc.gov/2023053989

24 25 26 27 28 LBC 5 4 3 2 1

First Edition

Greenwillow Books

To:

Dusty, The Giant, Macho Man, Mr. Perfect,

Animal and Hawk, The Rock, Jericho,

and all the rest who made me believe

A Professional Wrestling Glossary for Candy-Ass Jabronis

angle: a story
babyface/face: a good guy
bump: getting hit, kicked, or otherwise attacked in the ring that ends with you hitting the floor
candy-ass: idiot
closet champion: somebody who wins a championship belt but is too scared to defend it
feud: when two wrestlers (or groups of wrestlers) have an ongoing rivalry
grudge match: a match between two wrestlers with history—with a *grudge*
haircut match: loser gets the clippers!
heat: when fans are angry with a wrestler
heel: a bad guy
heel turn: when a face turns bad, usually unexpectedly
jabroni: idiot
jobber: somebody whose job is to lose
kayfabe: the willing suspension of disbelief (See: *Never break kayfabe.*)

receipt: a real punch or kick, usually in response to an accidental shot (i.e. *You paid for that kick, now here's your receipt.)*
screw job: an angle the fans don't like
parts unknown: a kayfabe location to create mystery around a wrestler's origin
pay-per-view: you pay money. You get to watch wrestling.
pop: when a wrestler comes out and gets applause
promotion: any company that puts on wrestling events
shoot: an unplanned, unscripted, or real-life occurrence in a match or story
stable: group of wrestlers managed by one person
suplex: wrestling move where you lift a person high in the air and then drop them on the mat
squared-circle: another name for the ring. Because it's a *ring*.
walk-in: walking into a match you're not supposed to be wrestling in. Big pop.
woo!: woo!
work: any pre-scripted wrestling storyline

AN OPENING PROMO

First things first, I wasn't suffering under some kind of delusion, because that was the first thing people thought when they heard about the Masked Man. And once it came out, people either started to back away slowly or said, "Julie, how did this . . . happen?" Everybody thought I was messing with them when I answered, but it was the truth.

Too much professional wrestling.

Was it concerning that I talked to an imaginary professional wrestler? Yes. Yes, it was. Trust me: I understood.

But listen, we all handled grief differently.

Still, I wasn't trying to mess with my line of therapists or the various "grief doulas" who had floated in and out of my life for the last three years, or especially my mom, who'd been diving hard into the world of crystals and self-help woo. Like I said, everybody grieved differently. For Mom, it was getting really into, like, kale smoothies. Who decided that it was out of bounds to converse with a hirsute, masked man known the world over for his brutality and for his ability to humble a grown man with a couple of sharp words?

We both lost Dad, one-two-three. Quick as a heart attack. That's all I was saying.

So, this wasn't a bit.

It wasn't a gimmick or an angle or a cry for help. It just happened.

All the therapists asked the wrong question, though. Had any of them been true believers, real fans, the real concern wouldn't be that I was delusional. No. Instead, it would've been . . . the Masked Man? That dude hadn't been seen—hadn't been relevant—in years.

The Man will not tolerate this disrespect, Juliana!

See that? That's how this has gone for the last few years. I think they called it intrusive thoughts, but the thoughts weren't exactly intrusive, and it'd be a lie to say I didn't know where he'd come from. The Man was my dad's favorite. And I guess that explains a lot.

Yes, he was probably the best wrestler ever to get on the mic, the sort of dude who could get a crowd whipped up with a single well-timed comeback. And yeah, he was so undeniably in on his own gimmick, you also had to kind of love him for it. While other people were ditching masks and feathered boas for cutoff jeans and leather vests, the Masked Man—the Maniac from Parts Unknown, the Violent Nightmare, the Picture of Aggression, the One True Devil—never wavered. Never took off the mask, not even when he was out in public for, like, the opening of a car dealership. And for that, you had to respect him.

Respect, candy-asses. You give it, or you get the big size-fifteen boot!

A quick word on masks.

Wearing a mask was about the closest thing to holiness you were going to get in professional wrestling—hell, even the regular world. The men and women who chose to wear masks were bound by a tradition bigger than themselves. Something that stretched all the way back to the Bible, when God showed up—wearing that angel mask—and took on poor old limping Jacob all night long.

There was one rule above all: you didn't take off the mask. Not ever. Not when some face tried to pull it off at the end of a grudge match, not when some kid wanted an autograph, or a sweetie in the crowd asked for a peck on the cheek. And for the real heads, the true believers, not even when a promoter said you'd gone stale and tried to get you to become the damn Repo Man or some other terribly generic gimmick.

Never going to happen, jabroni.

Nope, he switched territories. He created a new reign of terror. He stayed masked. He stayed the Man.

But like I said, nobody had seen or heard from the dude in decades.

Well, except for me.

And I couldn't get him to shut up.

Careful, jabroni . . .

And okay, fine, he might not be relevant, but he was still compelling. Every one of his matches, every promo, was marked by beautiful chaos. Unfortunately, it seemed I caught him on the slide into complacency, because he wasn't exactly interested in stomping out jabronis much these days. Sure, there were moments when I'd catch a glimpse of that fire—when he sounded ready to kick some candy-ass—but mostly, when he spoke to me, the Masked Man only cared about Orange Julius and the Mall of America.

The Masked Man has something to say!

So, anyway, nobody much worried about the Man these days, including Mom—even though I knew she still had all the therapists, the medication on speed dial. The most I got now was a quick breathing exercise followed by some time spent in child's pose.

Wait for ittttt. . . .

Still, I sometimes thought I should've given a better answer, if only to her. A quick conversation. Peace of mind to know that, fundamentally, I was okay.

Because if I had to explain it?

Like, really had to boil down the reasons why I spent most of the last three years in a daily dialogue with an irrelevant, reclusive, masked professional wrestler?

Wait for ittttt. . . .

He made me feel safe.

Let's go to Orange Julius. Boooooooom!

It sounded stupid, I knew this. But hearing him was a deep breath. A moment when I didn't have to do anything except agree that the Breathtaking One was the most overrated heavyweight champion of all time and say, Listen bro, we've already been to Orange Julius five times this week.

Say yes, Juliana.

CHAPTER ONE

The Mall of America was only fifteen minutes from my house, but when you walked through those doors, you might as well be in a different universe. It wasn't cool to be down with the M.O.A., especially if you'd spent your entire life in the Cities. And sure, I actually didn't remember it before the Mall sold out and let the theme park go all corporate, but real heads knew. We knew. It was a sprawling model of late-stage capitalism, but the Masked Man loved it. I was here four, five days a week.

I am a champion of spectacle.

That was an understatement, but we had a rhythm—show up just as the mall walkers were heading home, but before the middle school kids were unleashed, their parents a respectable but visible distance behind them. I started on the top floor, passing an increasing number of empty storefronts, down to the next—mostly regional stores and novelty shops. Every so often a weird pop-up would appear, shelves of flags and robotic dogs and squishy balls—flea market fodder that, in my opinion, didn't deserve an audience within the hallowed halls of the Mall.

Junk. That's what you're trying to say.

Anyway, a food court, a second food court—mini golf and a glimpse of the theme park—and then you were down to the main floors, both of which were proper cathedrals to the shopping gods. All the high-class places—video games, clothing, and one pricey jewelry store manned by an older gentleman who I sometimes made up stories about as I sipped my Orange Julius. How he carried on with the pointless endeavor of a mall-based jewelry store because it had once been the dream of his now-dead wife—

A tale for the ages, older than the Mall—perhaps even time—itself.

—which proved, most certainly, that I needed a life.

Anyway, finally on the bottom floor there it was—Orange Julius, tucked right in the corner, just on the other side of the escalator. Prime real estate, honestly. Because who could resist an Orange Julius after a long day of shopping for flags, body spray, and robotic hamsters?

Nobody, Juliana. That is the beauty of the Mall.

That's right. Nobody.

There wasn't a line—there never was a line—and, like always, Max was leaning on the counter, his head propped up by a hand. Lazily scrolling on his phone.

"Maximillian," I said, surprising him so much that he dropped his phone on the counter, watching helplessly as it slid toward me. Before it could fall to the ground, I caught it and smiled. He was only a few months younger than me, but he looked like he could still be in middle school. Small. Slight. I could take him. Nothing more than a buck-twenty-five soaking wet.

With some change left over!

A jabroni.

You said it, Juliana.

"Jesus, Julie. You realize you should, like, not just sneak up on people. And as always, just 'Max.' It's not short for anything."

I knew this. I also did not care.

"Sneak up? You're literally at work, Maximillian. And who names their son 'just Max'?"

"Greg and Kathy, that's who," he said, pulling his phone out of my hand.

I knew his parents as well as my own—they were nice, boring, perfect. And before Dad died, they would show up at our house for game nights, double dates—actual best friends, which put a lot of pressure on me and Max to keep the friendship going.

Still, despite knowing them so long that we might as well share DNA, what most surprised me was how unfazed Max was by their presence. They'd be fresh off sharing an Admiral's Feast at Red Lobster and think, "Hey, let's swing by to see the kiddo," which was totally a thing Greg would say. Most kids our age would be mortified to see Greg and Kathy rolling up on a Saturday night—peak time at the Mall—halfway finished with a forty-something date night.

But not Max. He'd stand there smiling and talking and

smiling some more until they left.

It wasn't the only thing I liked about Max, but it didn't hurt.

Max got to work making two Orange Julius originals—the orange monster, the OG, none of those premium fruit drinks for me and the Man. Max took this part of his job seriously, so much so that he refused to speak to me as he worked. When he first got hired, he'd been overly formal, pretending he didn't know who I was—all "Yes, ma'am" and such. But soon enough he calmed down, was able to talk to me like a normal human being. Even if he still took unusual pride in every smoothie he made. It was weird but put another check mark in the Max-being-too-good-for-this-world column.

I'll put a check in the candy-ass column, too!

Max turned around, two drinks in his hands, smiling as if this was the first time, back when I still in the throes of it all. When all I could do was show up and drink Orange Julius and lean against the concrete pillar at the corner of the storefront.

I took a sip of one drink. "So, did you ask out that girl from Hot Topic yet?"

He went red immediately and I tried to hide my smile with another pull from the big cup of Orange, nearly incapacitating myself when the sudden shock took over my brain. Max coughed and shrugged and fumbled with his phone before finally shaking his head and saying, "Dating is overrated. Aren't you the one who told me that?"

I set the cup of Orange Julius down and fixed my most devastating stare on Max. I didn't believe this for a second.

He's a candy-ass, boom!

I was messing with him, just a bit, so when he blushed again, unsure what to do with his hands, I felt guilty. Before I could say anything, a couple of skater kids went racing by—running and dropping onto their boards as they cackled at the out-of-breath security guards chasing them. I hopped up on the counter as they zoomed past, catching a wink from the shorter of the two.

When the excitement had passed, I took another sip of my drink and turned back to Max. "I'm just saying, don't give up. I'm sure there's a goth queen out there who wants to, like, hold your hand or something. Just go for it."

Max relaxed. He leaned across the counter, a crooked smile on his face, ready to give me the same business he'd been giving me half my life.

"Hold my hand? No necking? I mean, what about some good old-fashioned courting—hey, in the food court, maybe?"

"Oh God, you're right. You can find a girl who will—"

He held up his hand and stopped me before I could make it indecent. "I . . . get it. And I don't know. Maybe I'm just waiting for my moment."

I snorted.

"Well, I hope your goth queen gets a sudden urge for Orange Julius," I said. "Or at least, there aren't any more drive-by skateboard incidents. What is happening to our little local mall, Max?"

I hopped off the counter and grabbed the drinks.

"Uh, where are you going?"

I knew Max wanted me to stay tethered to the counter for one of our conversations that effortlessly moved from one topic to the next, only backing away when other customers approached. Maybe the biggest thing I'll miss when we both graduate and go our individual ways. But I wasn't going to think about that now.

"I need to go home and actually figure out my extended essay. Mr. Wentz wants to talk to me tomorrow, and I think he's on to me."

I raised both Orange Julius cups up, as if to toast Max as I walked away.

My Orange Julius was gone by the time I got to the truck. I tossed the empty cup into the back seat with at least ten others, and put the other one—melting now—into the cupholder, staring at it for a second, watching the condensation form on the side as the orange liquid thinned and thinned and thinned, until I shook myself out of the daze and looked around the empty parking deck, dark even though the sun was still hours from setting.

When I got home, I paused in the doorway of our house and wiped my mouth a few times to get rid of any rogue orange on my lips. Mom didn't approve of Orange Julius.

A lack of vision!

Still. When I was sure there wasn't a speck, I headed into the kitchen, where Mom was standing over a boiling pot of water and humming an indistinct melody—probably a chant, a mantra to calm the soul. She was really into chanting lately.

"Hey!" I called out, and Mom jumped.

"Julie! Where have you been?"

It wasn't a loaded question, not exactly, but it also wasn't an innocuous one. Ever since Dad died, Mom had an unusual interest in my daily movements. Something that went beyond normal parental concern. Part of it was anxiety, but a lot of it was her sudden anti-materialism stance (I was pretty sure I caught her looking up how to make herself a pair of pants last week), all of which meant the Mall was not her favorite place. And truthfully, it never had been. Dad was always the initiator of any trip to the Mall.

Mom seemed to be staring at my lips and I couldn't help myself, I licked them again.

"What's for dinner?" I said, hoping to distract her. Subterfuge. Mom gave me her long look, the one where her eyes flirt with an ever-so-brief roll before she turns to another activity, in this case pointing to the pot of boiling water.

"Baked ziti. Do you want to shred the cheese?"

I grabbed the grater and a block of mozzarella and got to work, letting the mindless task take me away for a few moments. Mom was humming again, definitely a chant, the whole scene surreal, as if somebody had taken a paintbrush and softened all the edges—a normal Monday night transformed into something that, like the chant, was both familiar and not.

The knock on the door came at the same time as the realization.

Normal. It felt like before.

I wasn't sure if I jumped because of that or because of the door, but Mom's eyes shot up, like, *Who could that be?* She wiped her hands on her apron—she was wearing an apron!—as she walked to the door. And trust me when I say that I knew who it was before I saw his face. His preternaturally chipper voice boomed through the house.

"Margaret! Look at that apron!" He laughed, somehow even more ecstatic than I thought was possible.

"Oh, Scott—what are you doing here?" I could hear the blush in Mom's voice, the awkward way she always said exactly what she was thinking. No filter, Dad had always said with a smile. "I mean, I'm happy to see you. But it's a surprise. A good one! Hey, Julie, Scott is here!"

Cool.

"Yeah, cool."

Scott was in yoga teacher training, a self-proclaimed ragamuffin who wore a beaded necklace with a half-moon charm around his neck. He'd retired from a corporate job maybe five years ago after "getting lucky" with crypto. He was always dressed in fabrics that allowed for better "flow," linen and such. The sort of guy who looked like he woke up and drank sunshine straight from the source. Always happy, always tan—yes, even in Minnesota—the kind of jabroni who would walk up to you and ask, without irony, how your energy was today.

You forgot that he's also a total candy-ass, Juliana.

Implied. But I said, "Hey," still holding the block of mozzarella, which I had intended to be a subtle sign—we're in the middle of dinner, *Scott.* Maybe come back, I don't know, *never*? But instead, it ended up being a classic blunder.

Because Scott motioned to the mozzarella and asked if—haha!—I carried it around with me wherever I went, and then Mom, casual as could be, was, like, "Why don't you join us? We're going to have too much either way."

I shot Mom my best look, sharp and out quick like a boot knife, but she didn't see or maybe couldn't see because of the glow from Scott's sparkling blue eyes, which I was pretty sure were fake. Contacts, something.

"It's not ready yet," I said, coming so close to mouthing, "Sorry . . ." all sarcastic, but Mom was already pulling Scott up the stairs and laughing as he grabbed the spare apron—my apron, which, sure, I'd never worn but there were rules, etiquette, and there he went tying it around his waist. And God, the way Mom was laughing, you'd think there was a comedy routine happening in our kitchen.

This guy.

Here's another thing about old Scott: he never stopped talking. Not as we finished boiling the noodles, or as we put the ziti together and shoved it into the oven. Scott was still talking as he whipped up a quick kale salad and told us about the spiritual-based, mindful-eating cleanse he was currently on, which would culminate—of course—with a yoga retreat that he really hoped would "manifest some tranquility in the world." He'd already knocked back half the salad by the time we finally pulled the ziti out of the oven, bubbling over with cheese and anti-tranquility goodness. If seeing me go to town on the ziti spoiled the zen in old Scott, I couldn't tell. He was just a constant fountain of words. Stories about camping in Bali, surfing in the Maldives. Words, all the words, woven together with an effortlessness that I have never had in my life.

Juliana . . .

The Man's nudge was two beats late. Scott had stopped talking, and he and Mom were staring at me.

"Huh?"

"Scott asked about your energy, honey."

I swallowed hard. There was no food in my mouth. I swallowed again anyway. Because what he really meant was: how was I doing. I never heard it as a question—always a statement. As if "how I am doing" hadn't been a constant grudge match for the last three years. Nobody wanted to hear that. They didn't want to know that I was still sad most days, still angry on more than I'd like to admit. And on the worst days, it felt like no time had passed at all. As if a faucet had been turned on and the handle ripped off. That, now, I was just used to a certain amount of running water.

"I'm working on a big essay for school," I said, taking a bite of ziti. "But you know, maybe I'll move some energy around later tonight. Keep myself fresh."

Juliana . . .

Scott gave me a patient smile and, to his credit, turned to Mom and said, "Well, I'm sure the ziti will help. Thank you for the wonderful dinner and the better company, Margaret."

He stood up, patted his stomach theatrically, even though it was as flat as the dining room table and all that dude had eaten was kale. Scott smiled one last time before following Mom to the door. I didn't move until Mom was back upstairs, looking rosy even though it wasn't that cold outside.

"I'm sorry," I said.

She cocked her head to the side. "What? Why?"

"I . . . don't know."

I felt deflated, the moon to Scott's eternal sun. Cold and empty—uninhabitable. Perhaps it was a reverse maternal instinct that made me ache inside. I knew she was happy. I knew she was trying to move forward. But I wasn't ready, and maybe I didn't want her to be ready, either, as terrible as that made me feel.

Mom sighed and reached over to pat my arm.

"I get it. I should've asked you if you were comfortable having him here."

She picked up the three plates and carried them to the kitchen as I watched, not saying another word.

CHAPTER TWO

Mr. Wentz taught Senior Philosophies, a class required for seniors at Central High School and one that left me wishing that all of school was more like this, more open-ended. Less directive. Other classes at Central gave a perfunctory nod to this sort of thinking. But Wentz took his teaching of this course as an almost solemn duty, a necessary counterbalance to the Christian schools in the suburbs that taught by asking kids questions like, "If you had two sins and Jesus took all of them away, how many sins would you have left?" Plus, he was a wrestling fan. A scholar, a historian, a true believer, known to thread in a story about some wrestler who nobody but I knew because it reminded him of, like, Emma Goldberg.

Anyway, I liked Philosophies. I liked Wentz. And at this point, as a senior, the rest of my courses, even if I got good grades, could kick rocks. They were filler, boxes to check to prove that I'd done the bare minimum. But this class somehow felt more real, which I realize is kind of ridiculous when compared to, say, math or whatever.

One plus one = shut up, nerd. Boom!

I liked having to think through the implications of what we say, what we think, and what we believe. I liked listening to sophomoric arguments made by seniors, people I'd known most of my life, but somehow had recently transformed into the sort of people I thought only existed in the suburbs. They believed in all of the pomp of graduation, that we weren't all living in some predetermined story.

You are nothing if not open-minded, Juliana.

So, the class was the tits—and before you get all worked up, just know that Max and I had a long conversation about how "the tits" was better than "the shit" because the scatological was gross and the only reason somebody wouldn't want to say "the tits" is because they're either a total prude or totally the patriarchy. So, Philosophies? The tits.

Philosophyyyyyyyyyyyyy!

Despite all this, Wentz—or I guess it was technically "the school system"—also had an expectation that we would "write a paper" to show that we "learned something" so we "could graduate." And let's just say that my topic—"On the Benefits of Never Breaking Kayfabe"—had gotten raised eyebrows from Wentz, who had said—and I quote—we could "do whatever we want, as long as it was important in our lives."

Anyway, Wentz liked to say that he saw potential in me, and that was always the kiss of death with a teacher. Especially with Wentz, because it meant he would call you into an early morning meeting like the one we were about to have and probably point to the other topics coming from the try-hards in our class, all of which made me so tired.

Religious cults.

War and PTSD.

The death penalty.

School shootings.

The problem of evil.

The one girl who was only allowed to wear long skirts who was most certainly going to choose "pro-life."

And fine, point conceded. It wasn't that any of them were unimportant, or even bad topics (well, except the whole I-can't-wear-pants-because-I'm-a-Christian-and-was-born-with-a-uterus girl), but they all felt . . . disconnected, somehow, from our actual lives. Impersonal. As if somebody had said, "Hey, don't focus on what you can control, but instead—focus on these global problems!" And, again, fine. But I wanted to write about something I actually believed in, and if that was a problem with the liberal elite at Central High School, well, let them riot.

Anyway, Wentz was sitting there staring at me, all happy-slappy, like he knew something I didn't, which of course was almost always true.

"What. God."

"There it is. There's that sunny disposition that makes me get out of bed each morning and think, 'I love teaching because of the impact I have on my students.'"

Sometimes Wentz said things that only made him laugh

and it was usually best to just chuckle along because, like I said, he could be kind of insufferable with all his positivity. He was still smiling, and it was like a goofy contagion. So I looked away and said, "I don't want to, like, write my paper about Amazon's effects on migrant workers in the Fernando Valley or whatever. I want to talk about the suspension of disbelief in professional wrestling—and you already signed off on it, so that's on you. No fair trying to take it away now."

I crossed my arms and everything. Wentz laughed.

"Oh no. This isn't about your extended essay. I have a feeling you're going to wish it was, though."

I looked at him hard, as if I could figure out his intentions simply by studying how the wrinkles in his face held the reminders of his smile. He pulled out a bright pink flyer and slid it across his desk. It was like a vampire being presented with a crucifix. I drew back, perhaps a little dramatically.

"Prom committee?" I asked. "Are you kidding me? No way."

"Hear me out, Julie."

This jabroni is about to get the big size-fifteen boot! To the face!

"You're about to graduate and I'm afraid you're going to miss out on the quintessential high school experience." I stared at him, which he ignored. "I was talking to your mom and—"

"Judas!" I said, reaching for my phone to text her as much. Wentz stopped my hand.

"It could be fun? And there's been some recent, uh,

drama. I think they could really use somebody with your specific personality."

"My personality? What exactly are you trying to say, Wentz?"

He sat up a little straighter and coughed.

"Are you saying I'm an asshole? Because it sounds like you're saying I'm an asshole."

Strong-willed, Juliana.

He coughed again. Fought off a smile. And then, finally, fixed his face with the familiar, "serious" teacher stare.

"Well, I'm not allowed to say that . . . exactly."

"Wentz, this is why you keep winning educator of the year."

"Seriously, though, Julie. You have a gift for cutting through the crap and getting things done. Do you disagree?"

I shrugged. I had always been intense, even in elementary school when Mom and Dad had been called to the school time and time again for various conversations about little Julie's penchant for being dramatic—for "threatening to introduce Timmy to the people's elbow" because he'd kicked me, which I still think he deserved, even if it was against six different school and district policies.

"What do I know about prom?"

"I'm sure about as much as me," he said. "I'm not that kind of gay man."

"I just . . . I have a lot on mind right now, Wentz."

I knew I'd made a mistake before the words left my

mouth. Mr. Wentz's entire demeanor changed, going from the playful, cool teacher to Concerned Adult, which was something I was so familiar with I could sense it coming like a trick knee senses a change in the weather.

"How are you doing? We haven't checked in lately."

It had been months since anybody had "checked in" with me, which made me wonder if I was suddenly putting off some kind of weird, anxiety pheromone or something. A beacon that attracted well-meaning adults like a swarm of bees to a pot of honey. First Scott, now Wentz.

"Fine, you know. Same as always."

"And you know . . ." He motioned as if somebody was sitting next to me. At first I didn't understand, and I looked to where he pointed, expecting to see somebody hidden under one of the desks. And then I realized.

Me, jabroni.

Right.

"Yeah, he's . . . also fine."

I could say this for Wentz, he got it—at least, as much as anybody could get it. He grew up watching the Masked Man. He understood the thrill of slowly, but ultimately, acknowledging the heel, the bad guy, was sometimes more exciting than the face, the good guy who always seemed to be smiling—who never hit you with a steel chair when your back was turned. But right then, I didn't want or need the real connection, the extra-special teacher treatment. So, I threw a reversal at him and started talking about the weather.

"It might snow again. It's almost May, Wentz. Minnesota forever."

"Well, that would be . . . inconvenient."

And so it went, back and forth, until other kids started arriving for class and he finally stood up and said, all official and really loudly, "Well, now that you're formally the newest member of the prom committee . . ."

I stood up, too, and said, "That so?"

"Yeah, because of all the slack I give you in my class."

"Extortion is probably in the student handbook," I said, walking toward my desk—turning my back on him mostly so I could hide my smile as he told me that I should check on that and get back to him. Before I got too far away, he said my name. Took a few steps toward me, so only I could hear him.

"Seriously, though. I think this will be good for you. Give it a try?"

After Wentz's class I walked out into the hallway, and I swore it was like somebody from central casting had planted the three girls in the hallway. The leader—there was always a leader—was younger than me by a year, maybe two. Who could keep track? Anyway, she turned to me, her practiced smile curved like a blade. Her words dipped in honey. Both of them sharp.

"Did you see?"

I shook my head.

Don't spook them, Juliana!

One of the pack, a blushing and doe-eyed girl, stepped out and handed me a flyer. She breathlessly said, "Look!"

It was moments such as these that defined us.

Juliana . . .

I'd play nice, but that seemed like something that would be narrated in this exact moment. Like I would look down at this piece of paper and everything would change. The music would swell. The credits were ready to roll. Suddenly I'd be okay. Healed. Whole.

But it was the same pink prom flyer Wentz had shoved at me—the theme of prom had just been announced. I turned around, expecting Wentz to be looking at me—he would have expertly engineered this exact moment. But he was excitedly talking to some kid about their extended essay.

My tongue was faster than my good sense so I said, "The theme is . . . enchanted gardens?"

The girls nodded, triumphant, in unison, a collective being of enthusiasm and energy.

There was a time—when the Man and I first teamed up—that I would've dropped a promo on these three girls. The Man, holding the mic for me as I totally eviscerated the one who'd handed me the flyer, still standing with her hand out. Back then I could get away with it. The raw anger, the deep loss. All of it bubbling up into frenetic words that dropped onto people like an elbow from the top rope. Right after Dad died, every do-goodie-two-shoes wanted to connect. People felt obligated to be nice, I guess, to find me and ask me to sleepovers. I could see it in their eyes, like asking me to come to the roller rink would somehow save me.

Don't dismiss a good roller rink.

"Uh, thanks. This is . . . exciting."

Especially if it has a DJ.

I stuffed the flyer into my pocket and stepped around the group who went back to their cooing over the prom announcement. As soon as I got past them, something dropped inside me. A brick tossed through a window, crashing its way through my body. A realization that, maybe, I would've been just as excited about enchanted gardens once. Maybe I would've loved being on the prom committee—how could I even know at this point?

There aren't enough live DJs at roller rinks.

And suddenly, people were everywhere—laughing, excited—and all I could feel was red, the thermostat rising, burning me up, building and building like water behind a pinched hose until I couldn't stop the tears, big and fat and hot under my eyes.

And then I ran.

I ran to the far end of the school, the bathroom where people smoked, somehow avoiding teachers. It was empty, and I ran to the closest stall, opened the door, and collapsed to the floor, telling myself not to cry—don't you cry.

Of course, everything came out.

Three years of grief that never seemed to empty itself.

Three years of this same detachment from everything, spending so much energy trying to be okay—which was deeply exhausting. A weariness that settled on your bones.

Three years.

Juliana?

Three years of thinking I was okay only to discover I'd been running, sprinting, so hard the entire time. So fast that I could forget until I hit a brick wall and came crashing into the realization that I didn't feel any different.

Are you okay?

Not for three years.

In the time it took me to get off the floor, tell myself I was finally okay—this was the last time, that same lie—the entire school had made a pact to collectively lose their shit about the prom theme. Above me the bell rang, meaning I was officially late to my next class. But that didn't make me walk any faster. I was alone in the hallway, and it felt like traveling against the current of this dimension. The soft droning of the classrooms buzzed around me as I moved silent and unnoticed.

At some point Dad had given me a dusty sci-fi novel about a person who lived backward, against time. He was excited about it, spent a solid hour telling me all kinds of . . . trivia? I only made it a few pages before going back to the Baby-Sitters Club books Mom had dropped in my lap that same day—both of us sharing a wink at Dad's expense. Still, even though I hadn't finished the book, the idea had stuck with me. Mostly how difficult it would be to live backward, to always be one step closer to being completely alone.

I turned down the hallway to my next class and jolted to

a stop. An odd group of students were bickering like a bunch of children at recess. Three girls and two boys holding skateboards—who seemed out of place in every way. Two ladders stood on either side of the hallway and a banner ("ENCHANTED GARDENS!") drooped between them, effectively blocking my path.

Rebuffed by enchanted gardens once again!

For a second I considered turning around—waiting out the entire next period in a bathroom. I was already late. But then one of the girls, a senior with perfect blond hair and just enough makeup to accent her blue eyes, turned and called out to me.

"Hey! Can you help us? We're a couple hands short."

"We told you we would help," the shorter of the two skater boys said.

"You are not on the committee," the blonde said.

"Did we fill out the paperwork?" the boy asked his friend. His friend nodded. "Does it look like they need help lifting this heavy-ass banner?"

His friend nodded again, smiling.

The girl ignored them and lifted the sagging middle, which looked heavier than it should be. I took a handful, and the weight pulled my arms down momentarily, surprising me.

"Did they run out of regular paper?" I said without thinking.

The two skater guys laughed. "Here we are being all noble, trying to be all chivalrous and shit—full of school spirit! Trying to help plan the prom! And what do we get?"

"Disrespect," the taller one said.

"You hate to see it."

They slapped hands.

The girl grimaced and then fought to bring back her smile. She leaned close, her voice becoming an agitated but conspiratorial whisper. "First, ignore them—they are not on the committee. Second, I ordered the wrong type of banner—all-weather, I guess."

"Well, better safe than sorry?" I whispered back.

Nice one, jabroni.

The girl laughed and said, "I'm Briar, by the way—you are?"

"Julie. I was actually just conscripted onto the—"

Briar cut me short. "Hey, Margo, lift it up a little on your end."

Margo, with great effort, lifted up her side of the banner, latching the metal ring onto a hook on the wall. On the other side, a girl named Penelope gave it her all, finally hooking the banner and looking down at Briar with nothing short of contempt.

"I'm sorry! I just didn't want the stupid thing getting torn down. You know people are going to jump up and slap it."

"Boys. Boys are going to slap it," Penelope said.

The two skater boys started pushing each other and saying, "Slap it, yeah."

"That sounded . . . way grosser than we intended it,"

Briar said. "I am not going to another HUMP session."

I literally dropped the banner. The two boys, who'd been attempting to slap each other on the ass, stopped and stared at Briar.

Briar sighed. "Abstinence curriculum at my church. Well, former church, I guess. Whatever. It stands for "Helping U Maintain Purity." Or HUMP, which was definitely unintentional," Briar said, her voice dropping a bit now that everybody was paying attention to her.

Hump! At church!

Margo lifted the banner up a little higher until it stretched perfectly across the hallway ceiling. "Okay, Penelope, tie it off."

"I never HUMP-ed at church," I said cautiously.

There was a beat, a respectful moment of silence perhaps, immediately followed by laughter loud enough that I was sure a teacher would be in the hallway soon.

"Well, thank God for that, Julie!" Briar raised her eyebrows at me. "You don't want to fall in with the wrong crowd!"

The two skater boys collapsed into each other. The shorter one gave me a nod of appreciation. I wasn't sure what to do with myself, but the energy had changed subtly. Both of Briar's friends went tense. Briar noticed and, I thought, resented the way they were avoiding looking at her. I was already a couple steps down the hallway when Briar said my name.

"Hey—thanks for the help! See you around?"

I paused. Briar looked like any number of the other girls at this school—pretty, obviously from money. But it was as if she were outlined in silver, highlighted somehow, because while it was obvious that the others were trying hard, everything about Briar was effortless.

"Yeah, I mean, I guess I'm your newest member of the prom committee."

She looked genuinely excited. But it wasn't her who spoke. The shorter of the two skater boys pumped a fist in the air and said, "Us, too! Let's go!"

"They are not on the committee," Briar said one final time before I turned and walked away.

Max had missed half of the school day for a dentist's appointment, so after school I went straight to the mall and walked around for an hour before he finally showed up for his shift.

"Took you long enough," I said.

Max stared at me, tying his apron, before he finally said, "You do know that anybody here is qualified to make you an Orange Julius. Like, literally that's what they're here to do. Marvin has been here all day."

I shrugged and waved to Marvin, who was hanging up his apron. Marvin worked multiple part-time jobs, presumably for the different discounts, and lived in a house that had been gifted to him by a well-off parent ten or twenty years ago.

"You have a special way about you, Maximillian. A soft touch with the blending machine."

That made him laugh, which always felt like a win. "Soft touch. Good Lord."

And without another word, he made the two Orange Juliuses. When he finished, two cups in his hands, Max smiled big, proud—like some kind of goofy kid. But it was all a distraction.

"So, Wentz told me the big news," he said, smirking. "Enchanted gardens forever, Julie."

"Effing Wentz," I said, taking the cups. "Isn't that against FERPA or something?"

"I don't think your involvement in prom is protected by the . . . Family Educational Rights and Privacy Act."

"Well, if not that, then what."

Enchanted gardens!

Max leaned against the counter and we both stared out at the empty mall, me drinking my Orange Juliuses. At this time of year, the Mall was admittedly rather pedestrian. A few scattered chairs left over from a spring choir concert the night before. Nothing like when the Christmas decorations were up and the place truly felt alive, still magical even though we were supposed to have aged out of that opinion. Kids running from store to store, waiting until it was time for them to sit on Santa's lap, a mouth full of Christmas lists and dreams. The pumped-in Christmas music, just barely audible but still strangely comforting. Even fake snow, falling from the ceiling in the rotunda. Nobody could argue that during the holidays, the Mall held a sort of beautiful expectation that was rare anywhere else.

"Oh! I can't believe I forgot! I blame you, of course, with all your . . . anyway." Max reached behind his apron and pulled out a wadded collection of papers from his pocket. He unfolded the pages, smoothed it a few times on the counter, and pushed it toward me.

The first page was just a string of threaded comments from an Internet wrestling forum.

"You printed the Internet," I said. "Congratulations."

Annoyance flickered over Max's face like a wayward cloud. But he rallied and with a flourish unveiled the last page from the stack.

"My dentist let me print it out." Before I could comment he said, "Just read it."

A picture of a respectable, if not at one time attractive, older man stared back at us. He looked like he used to play football but now sold cars or perhaps insurance. Good hair but thinning. Huge smile. Enough bulk to be menacing if he wanted but with more Scott energy than anything else. It didn't help he was holding a book called *Dancing Into the Unknown*.

Look at this broken-down, candy-assed jabroni.

Max or this guy? It made me laugh.

"You really need to stop with the self-help books," I said.

Max stared at me, obviously disappointed. "You're losing street cred in real time. Right here."

I was about to make another comment, something about not being on top of the pseudo-spiritual grift in the way he or Mom was, but something stopped me.

You might recognize him with my boot up his ass, Juliana.

It was the shadow of a scar on the man's forehead, a life of being opened up by razor blades in the name of keeping it real. I imagined that generous smile slowly turning into a sly grin, followed by a flat-mouthed grimace. The arms, crossed in front of his barrel chest instead of giving us a big thumbs-up.

"Holy shit. That's . . ."

The Breathtaking One. What a stupid name.

"And guess who used his influence at the Mall to get two passes for his book signing in the rotunda?"

I couldn't stop myself from reaching over the counter and pulling Max into a hug. He squirmed at first but eventually relaxed, until he finally said, "Okay, okay. What are my ladies going to think?"

"Your ladies, okay. Calm down."

But I didn't take the ribbing any further, not even to qualify that he couldn't work up the gumption to talk to his "lady," singular, at Hot Topic, because I was transfixed by the picture on the paper. It was embarrassing that I didn't recognize him right away. Especially since I took it really hard when the Breathtaking One finally beat the Masked Man after years of loaded boots, referee chicanery, and every heel trick the Man had used on this once-pretty buffoon. The tears surprised my dad, who hadn't exactly been thrilled to see the Man go out on such a high-profile loss, either.

Breathtaking? Please. Look at that mug.

Still, as far as foils went, the Breathtaking One was about

as good as there was. He had swagger. He wore expensive suits and strutted around the ring. And he antagonized the Masked Man—and by default, his fans—enough that the line between good guy and bad guy was blurred. Since retiring from wrestling, he'd made the turn to self-help and mall-based psychology—Mom even came home with one of his books, like, "This is a wrestler!" Tapping the cover, all proud of herself for making the connection. And I hadn't been able to stop myself, being, like, "I know! I hate him!" Mom laughed me off, but you had to choose a side and Dad and I'd always been with the Man.

Thank you, Juliana.

There really wasn't ever a better bad guy, the sort of heel who had no problem secretly putting lead into the bottom of his boot—don't question it, just enjoy the ride—and delivering a kick to the jaw that could make you feel the bones breaking. I hated him. I loved him. My affection was a slow burn, but not my dad. He always claimed the Man was a throwback to the old-school heels before his time. The ones who wouldn't take a face turn and become a good guy because being a heel was nothing short of a calling.

"Do you remember when Adrenaline did the whole storyline where Breathtaking was supposedly going to lure the Masked Man out of retirement?" Max asked. "How excited we were?"

Adrenaline had always been a niche wrestling outfit, the only place where you could still see old-school, legitimate wrestling these days. Of course, there were other promotions, other outfits that were glitzier or tried to steal the championship belt, but there was something about Adrenaline—about its loyalty to past talent, to the history of the stories it had told, that made its fans loyal and rabid.

Adrenaline remains undefeated, Juliana.

"Uh, yes." I laughed.

"Instead, he showed up and had a match with that guy—the Butcher. Do you remember him?"

"Why must you disrespect me?"

The Butcher was a large man who wore only an apron, or so it seemed to our kid eyes when we watched. There was a lot of blurring. So much blurring.

This is the beauty of Adrenaline.

"The angle was that Butcher wants to bring back the Masked Man to help him woo Cherry Bomb, who, naturally, isn't going to go out with him because he's, you know, a large man in nothing but an apron. Which, admittedly, is one of the more troubling stereotypes."

"It's theater. It's not real life," I said. "Or maybe it's more real that we want to admit because it is so obviously wrong at times, and it's actually one big critique of reality! Thanks for coming to my extended essay."

That's right, jabronis!

Max blinked.

"Anyway, listen—the turn was when the Butcher realized that he didn't need to intimidate women to get them to love him and so, even though it was his idea, but you know, whatever, the Butcher slams the Breathtaking One through the announcer's table and it all ends with the Butcher declaring his love for Cherry and them getting married the next week."

A classic. Well-done, Adrenaline.

"And the Masked Man never showed up," I said. It was one of the more disappointing emotional manipulations in my life. He'd been gone for a while, but that was how it worked—anybody could walk through those curtains at any time.

If you watch wrestling long enough, you come to expect the beats—you know the script, even if you don't want to. You can see the storylines developing weeks in advance. But damn, I thought the Man was coming back. I really did. Wrestling does that; it creates weird hope—hope that can be extracted out, squeezed into other places in your life. So when he didn't show, a small part of that hope vanished. He wasn't ever coming back.

Max's energy shifted, just enough to notice when he tapped the paper one last time and said, "Well, I thought it would be nice."

I came home to a note from Mom saying she'd gone out to dinner with Scott and there were leftovers in the fridge—Get your homework done!—and because I'm such a good daughter I dropped my bag on the floor and headed straight back to Mom and Dad's room and opened the closet door.

You could still smell him. It was a mixture of old cologne and clothes Mom refused to donate—a collection of ratty

T-shirts that I adored. Sometimes I'd go into the closet to just sit there. To feel closer, if only by whatever trick my brain was pulling on me. In the beginning, when Mom was really worried about me, I always had an out, a way to make her feel better if she found me sitting there.

Oh yeah, let's do this.

Dad was not a believer in the internet, at least that's what Mom and I would say whenever he'd go fishing under the television cabinet for one of the countless VHS tapes—*VHS tapes!*—that he'd collected through the years, full of random cartoons and videos from MTV, weird commercials he said he didn't want to forget, and—the true gold—a lifetime of Adrenaline matches.

"All this stuff is probably on YouTube," I would tell him. But secretly, I loved coming home to find him setting up the VCR, Mom laughing as she told him he'd been born in the wrong generation. The hum of the machine. The way the tapes would start out fuzzy, then clear up. That sudden burst of sound.

It really is the only way to watch.

I didn't remember when Mom moved the VHS tapes into the closet—another thing she couldn't bear to get rid of, I guess. A way of tapering off him.

I opened the box and pulled out the first tape, squinting to see the faded writing on the spine: "Saturday Main Event, 1998." The next one was nearly indecipherable in the low light of the closet, so I set it aside. I already knew what I was looking for. When I found it, I stood up and made my way to the living room. Once I'd gotten the VCR set up, I popped in the tape and waited for the television to fill the darkening room with light.

The opening of "Stand Tall at the Mall" was, by all accounts, a total classic. It started with flying through space as the Classic Adrenaline logo dropped out of the solar system above and was knit together by lasers.

Lasers.

And if that wasn't enough, soon your ears were getting tickled by some sweet, soft jazz saxophone—the kind of business that would make you fall in love with a complete stranger. All of this built toward the big reveal—a mall. The Mall. Until then, every wrestling event I'd seen had occurred at stadiums and arenas, all of them impossibly grand and filled with smoke, like every adult and child in the place had been tasked with hotboxing the venue before the main event could begin. But this was in a place I knew. A place I'd been. I could see the cookie shop, the bookstore—Orange Julius. And that was almost as important as the matches. At least, until the Man faced off against the Breathtaking One and The Legend—when the entire world would stand still, just for a moment, just enough that you knew nothing was ever going to be the same.

Of course, nobody knew this would come to be considered the best match of all time. Or that half of the undercard would turn out to be deadbeats and derelicts, outing themselves as incompatible with decent society. Once, when I looked up one particularly problematic wrestler—the Mad Dog, who wore dog collars and barked at the crowd—Dad said that maybe that's the problem with heroes. Anybody who lived long enough would disappoint you. Anybody who lived that large would ultimately fall. They taught you regret. Even if they were responsible for so much more in your life.

Once the show started, I couldn't help but marvel at how much the Mall had changed. The bones were the same, of course, but it was like seeing an old picture of your parents—different hair and outdated outfits. Even the wrestling was different, matches front to back, with none of the modern walk-ups or backstage interviews to slow the show down. I let it drone on in front of me, mouthing the words of the announcers, Elephant Typhoon and Robbie "The Hyena" Brainerd, as they articulated the ups and downs of every match, the regret and the outrage—the vindication and the glory.

An inspiration to generations.

In all honesty, I couldn't tell you what actually made the match so important—why it gripped Dad, so many others, the way that it did. He was there, of course. And sometimes I would find myself watching the crowd—looking for him, instead of paying attention to the match. To see if his face was just as excited as it was when we watched the tape together. Honestly, I just enjoyed watching him watch the dusty tape. The way he physically reacted, as if he was being thrown around the ring with these overgrown men. I cared because he cared, which always struck me as a good definition of love.

I watched the match—scanning the crowd for a glimpse of his face, despite never seeing it before—rewinding it three times before I heard Mom's keys in the front door. A moment of panic struck briefly as I looked at the two empty Orange Julius cups, the shadows of professional wrestling flashing against the walls of our living room like police lights.

No candy-asses allowed!

Still, I didn't move—not when the door opened or when Mom called out my name, or when she came into the living room and found me, the lights from the television on her face showing me exactly how she felt, how worried she still was, even now. How, maybe, she had just wanted to come in to tell me about her date with Scott—whatever bougie health restaurant he'd found on the foodie blogs he followed.

Instead, I kept my eyes on the screen, waiting for Mom to say something. As though it were some perverse test I kept springing on her—show me how much you loved Dad, how much you still do. We stayed in that static moment for what felt like hours. Unable to move, to speak. Frozen in time the way the Breathtaking One was as the Masked Man stalked toward him for another strike with the metal chair.

Mom came to the couch and sat down, gently lifting my head until it rested on her lap. We watched the entire match. The next hit with the metal chair. The inexplicable comeback by the Breathtaking One. The way the Man was almost unmasked, saved at the last second by Big-time Bill. We didn't say a word until the Man went running through the crowd, still anonymous, and the crowd was, once again, unsure if it should be upset or relieved.

And just like that. A flawed legend was gone again.

The credits rolled and rolled and rolled until the tape finally clicked off, and Mom moved a strand of hair out of my face and said, "I love you, Julie."

CHAPTER THREE

The next morning I felt as if I'd been folded in half and left in a box for the entire night. When Mom said hello, I grunted and left it at that. Mom sat down at the kitchen table, both hands on her coffee cup, and took a few sips before she said, "So, I've got some news I wanted to share with you. It's about Scott. And me. You remember that yoga retreat that he was talking about? The one that he was hoping would, I don't know, help manifest tranquility or something?"

This time I groaned loudly. "I don't understand what you see in this guy."

Mom stared at her coffee and very calmly said, "He's nice to me, Julie. You don't know how hard this is."

Mom had always been traditionally beautiful, traditionally popular. I liked to think it was sort of a coup that Dad—a dissident, long-haired commie and unrepentant professional wrestling head—had somehow grabbed her attention. There was no question that they had loved each other passionately, but there were moments when the way they saw the world did not match.

Give her a break, Juliana.

"I just don't see it. That's all."

Mom nodded.

"You sound just like your father," she said quietly. "Do you know that he didn't want to have flowers at our wedding because, in his mind, they all seemed to indicate 'some kind of message'? Don't ask, because I still have no idea what he was talking about or what political message purple asters were supposedly putting out into the world."

She laughed once, staring deeper into her coffee and letting the silence of the room grow until she continued, "Heh. I haven't thought about that in a long time."

"Anyway. Scott wants me to go with him. On the retreat. And I want to go . . . but I want to make sure you would be okay. Alone, over the weekend." She paused, took a sip of coffee, and looked at me over the lip of the mug.

We should throw a party.

"Where are you guys going?" I asked, trying to buff any aggression, any annoyance from the words.

"The North Shore. Grand Marais—good energy up there, you know." She smiled weakly. "No comments, please."

Mom didn't say anything else, just took another drink of her coffee and then stood up, patting me on the shoulder as she passed by and made her way down the hallway to get dressed for work.

Mom was still getting ready when somebody knocked on the door, seven knocks in that familiar pattern, the one that Scott always used and then proceeded to Scottsplain how it actually came from an old song called "Shave and a Haircut, Two Bits." When I opened the door, Scott was liquid sunshine. The smile, a thousand volts. Cranked up to eleven with the knob broken off.

"Well, must be my lucky day," he said, all teeth and tan and breathable yoga pants. I called for Mom, then Scott got a reflective look on his face and his voice dropped, just enough that it put me on alert.

"Hey—so, I was talking to your mom, and I just want to make sure everything is okay."

Yes, how are you?

"Got conscripted onto the prom committee. You know how that goes."

Scott, in fact, didn't, so I smiled bigger, hoping to build a wall of sandbags to stop the coming tide of emotion. But unlike the tides, there was no way of knowing when the waters would surge toward me, grabbing my entire body and threatening to pull me into a sea of devastation that, years later, shouldn't be so deep. Waters I never saw coming, leaving me blinking and blinking and blinking, anything to push back every bit of emotion.

I tried to think of something happy.

The time we went to Dave & Buster's, a restaurant for adults who still wanted to believe in Chuck E. Cheese. Still wanted the thrill of eating fried food and playing video games, in tests of not-so-much strength as luck, in winning only kitsch, only trash.

Now this *is a good memory, Juliana.*

"Your mom told me you were having a rough time—missing your dad."

One does not need to be grieving to enjoy professional wrestling, Scott. *Tell him that for me, Juliana.*

I stood there, unresponsive. Unreadable. I thought about my dad trying again and again to win some stupid stuffed Pokémon for me. He was usually preternaturally good at those sorts of games, but that night he'd easily dropped a hundred bucks on something he could've gotten for twenty online. Eventually he'd slipped the clerk a bill and I walked out with it, maybe happier than I've ever been.

"She told me you were watching some of his old . . . home movies?"

Home movies? This aggression will not stand!

"They're wrestling tapes," I managed. "Professional wrestling."

Scott looked momentarily surprised, which I guess meant that Mom hadn't told him about her former husband's passion—an eternal embarrassment that she could never truly bring herself to hate. For some reason, her not sharing this part of him with Scott felt like she still loved him. Of course she still loved him. I knew that. And I knew that moving on wasn't mutually exclusive. I just didn't know how long a heart might hold on to love, even if mine was turning it into a marathon.

"Well, I can't say I know much about professional wrestling," Scott said, laughing. "But it strikes me that this was something you two shared—something that's still important to you?"

I nodded again.

Show him the tapes, Juliana. That will open his chakras!

Before I could say anything else, Mom yipped, a noise that was obviously excitement but also came from a guttural, almost mystical place. A sudden outburst that immediately mortified me, for the implications of this weekend retreat. And also, maybe, because even on his best days, Scott was a solid C- on all fronts and didn't merit this sort of response.

"What are you doing here!"

"Thought I'd take my girl out to breakfast," Scott said, sweeping Mom into his arms.

Mom gave me a look, like *Can you believe this?*, and I shot her one back, like, *What a guy!* And I didn't even roll my eyes, though I desperately wanted to. Because, love.

This candy-ass does seem to make her happy.

"On that note, I'm going to school."

"Do you want us to drive you?" Mom asked as she gave Scott a quick peck on the cheek. "Hey! You could go in late and join us! Both girls at breakfast!"

Mom glanced at Scott, and he nodded without a beat, which I guess counted for something. A point for Scott, fine. Still, I didn't know if I could spend another minute, let alone an entire meal, watching them play footsies and gazing into each other's eyes like a couple of love-starved kids.

"No, I'm good. But thanks."

Before they could say anything else to me, I was out the door.

• • •

I wasn't two steps into school when the PA system crackled, and the excited voice of the principal welcomed the students to another day at Central. I waved at Ms. Anne, the receptionist, and she smiled and pointed at her wrist because I was late once again, but I was too focused on Briar's banner—still hanging, albeit with a slight sag, most definitely the result of slapping.

Slap it!

I got to class just as the announcements were ending, and as soon as Wentz saw me, he said, "Late to class, but early to your presentation, Julie."

I stood there for a moment, watching Wentz smile like he knew how I'd spent the evening when, yeah, technically I knew the presentations were happening today. And in that little smile—maybe I'm projecting—I could also see him saying, "Maybe watching wrestling tapes isn't preparing for a presentation, Julie."

Wentz, you jabroni.

I couldn't tell if it was adrenaline, or simply the challenge, but something switched inside me and I dropped my bag, casual like, on the ground next to the podium set up in front of the class. Whatever bravado had carried me through the process of choosing our extended essay topic—telling myself and any student or teacher who would listen that all of this was another checklist on the fast, downward slope to graduation—was gone almost as soon as I gripped the sides.

Don't let these jabronis intimidate you, Juliana!

I cleared my throat, nodded once, and then looked at Wentz in hopes that he might throw me a life preserver—get back to your seat, you old so-and-so. That sort of thing. Instead, he smiled again, and I swore I'd never hated anybody more in my life. I cleared my throat again. Somebody chuckled in the back. I would end them, I thought, scanning the crowd.

A loaded boot to the jaw for them, dear.

I cleared my throat a third time and now even I was ready to laugh at how ridiculous this was going to be. Professional wrestling. I might as well not be allowed to wear pants to school because of my uterus.

"The title of my extended essay is: 'On the Benefits of Never Breaking Kayfabe.'"

There was a beat, followed by a nervous chuckle. A few more. I've never really cared about what people thought about wrestling. Not really. If anything, when you realized you were in the presence of another fan, it was like found money. Shared membership in a secret club. But for some reason it felt like I was in the middle of the ring, the life slowly being drained from my entire body. A sleeper hold, set in deep. The referee raising my hand, letting it drop like dead weight.

Just tell them why this is important.

People were mumbling to one another now, perhaps wondering if I was going to run out of the room. They, of course, knew my entire story—or thought they did. The broken girl. The fatherless girl. The one who needed kid gloves. Even Wentz looked worried. His mouth opened like he was going to grant me a reprieve.

My hand was lifted up a second time, and it dropped a second time.

Talk, jabroni.

My hand raised a third time. Once again, it started to fall—

But wait!

A sudden jolt of energy!

The hand, fighting against gravity. Could it stay in the air? Could this be?

Could this be?!

"In wrestling, *kayfabe* is about something fake being portrayed as real."

A cough. The faint sound of somebody tapping on the screen of their phone.

"But, like, what if we were still allowed to believe in things that weren't real?" I continued. "And what if kayfabe made them more real?"

Ahem!

I half expected somebody to nod in the back row, to start a slow clap in recognition that I'd cracked the code—liberated them from a reality lacking imagination and, instead, invited them into the childlike wonder of still believing. Of not breaking kayfabe.

Instead, somebody's phone went off and Wentz fussed about it for a few seconds before turning back to encourage me to go on.

"I guess I just believe there's still some mystery to be

eked out between the turnbuckles. Uh, like, encouraging us all to still believe. Or whatever. Let's not just give up on things we love. You know?"

Get some, jabronis!

Wentz looked at me and I thought I caught a sympathetic smile before he said, "Peter, let's go. You're next."

I'd been staring at my phone for five minutes, wondering if I could really turn any of this into an actual extended essay or if I should just plan to be a fifth-year senior, my lunch getting cold as hell, when Briar walked up and sat down.

"Hey! Julie! What are you doing?"

I stared at her, dumbfounded.

"Somebody slapped the banner."

Briar looked at me, confused, but then it clicked, and she laughed.

"Well, somebody stole it. So, turns out, slapping wasn't the biggest concern, I guess."

These jabronis have no respect.

"Who steals a banner?" I asked, thinking primarily about the size of the thing. Not to mention the weight. It was huge and heavy. "And then, like, what do you do with it?"

"All great questions," Briar said, sighing and unwrapping her sandwich from the cellophane packing. I hadn't eaten lunch with anyone other than Max in years, and this block he was trying to convince Senor Anerano that he shouldn't fail Spanish. I was ready for it to be me and a book and my earbuds, drowning everything out. So when Briar said, "Oh, do you mind?" I shook my head, because what else was I going to do?

"Anyway, we'll discuss it at our next prom committee meeting, okay? And no matter what you might hear, people are really excited about the prom theme," she said, taking a bite of her sandwich. "I mean, it's probably self-serving for me to mention that since I came up with it but, you know, the excitement is palpable. Right?"

It was more words than anybody, outside of a teacher, Max, or my mom, had said to me in longer than I could remember. Also, I wasn't exactly sure about enchanted gardens as a theme. So, I nodded, chewed, and nodded some more as Briar kept talking about the committee.

"It's a huge responsibility," she said, before getting suddenly embarrassed. "You probably think this is stupid."

"What? No."

Briar studied my face and said, "It's just—I don't know—I want it to go off without a hitch."

"It's prom," I said. "It's not like anybody is going to protest it. There was that one lady at Holy Angels, I guess."

Briar stiffened. "Yeah. I . . . remember."

"I mean, what did they think was going to happen? The king and queen would get crowned and then suddenly everybody was going to be naked?"

Briar shrugged and looked down at her sandwich, which made me feel awkward.

"All I'm saying is, I think Jesus has bigger problems. And prom at Central? That's a cakewalk."

Briar seemed to breathe and then she laughed once.

"You . . . don't know how helpful that is. Hey, what are you doing after school today?"

Orange Juliuuuuuusssss.

At first I was afraid she was going to call an emergency meeting of the prom committee but before I could say, "Nothing," she said, "We should hang out!"

"Uh, hang out?"

"Yeah, what do you usually do after school?"

Adreeeeennnnnnaaaaaallllllinnneeeee.

"I don't know. I usually, uh, go to the Mall?"

Briar slapped the table, hard. "Oh! I need to get some shoes! We're doing this. I'll drive!"

And just like that she was gone in a puff of smoke, chaos, and perhaps glitter.

I saw Max walking to the only class we shared, language arts, and he immediately noticed something about my face, my body language. He spent the entire class staring at me like he knew something, which was really annoying, and even though I tried my best to ignore him, I couldn't help but check to see if he was still watching me every few minutes. When the bell rang, he came straight to me.

"What?"

"Nothing." He laughed. "You look like you saw a ghost."

I shook my head and even I could tell how anxious I looked. It made him laugh harder. "Did you get asked to prom or something?"

"What? God. No. Don't put that evil on my life."

I started walking, fast, and Max double-timed it to keep up with me. "When you come to the Mall tonight, we can work up the definitive list of questions for the Breathtaking One's appearance."

Question one: What's it like to be a candy-ass?

I laughed.

"What's more ethically questionable—hitting somebody with a metal chair or shilling self-help books?"

"Okay," Max said. "Let's not ask that question."

"My guess is that we'll be the only people there wanting to know about his ascension from the Mid-South promotion to Adrenaline and then Old Japan."

Max shrugged but didn't say anything else as we came to the top of the stairs that marked where we would go our separate ways for the rest of the day.

"Hey, you sure you're good?"

"People have been asking me that a lot lately," I said. "I must be giving off a scent."

"Just the normal ones," Max said.

I went to hit him but he was diminutive, like a child, so I missed, and he cackled as he jumped down the stairs—swearing that he loved me.

CHAPTER FOUR

I don't know why but I fully expected to walk right out the school doors and onto the sidewalk without even a whiff of Briar. But there she was in the parking lot looking more excited than ever. Hands above her head. A quick, unexpected, and inexplicable flex. Followed by what can only be described as a top-of-her-lungs, unabashed, enthusiastic war cry—"Mall of America!"

Woo! Let's go!

Which was not my reaction. By the time I reached Briar, I had managed to cover up my embarrassment, not that she noticed. She talked nonstop, obviously excited, and when we pulled into the Mall's parking lot, I knew perhaps everything there was to know about Briar. Her friends call her Bri—and so could I—along with the details of her family, the colleges she hoped to attend, the ones that would be good enough, and the fact that she was coming off a rather devastating breakup to a rather bland-sounding boy who went to her former school, Holy Angels.

"He wants to be a youth pastor," she said. "So, there was

lots of strumming guitars and praying."

"I could hook you up with my friend Max," I said. "He works at the Mall. Orange Julius."

It came out before I really thought of the implications.

"Like, the shake place?"

"Shake place"? How dare you.

"It's more . . . smoothies."

"Oh, we should get one!"

I take that back. I like this Bri. She is a good influence.

It was weird to be at the Mall with somebody else, not to go through the regular ritual of starting at the top floor and moving slowly downward. And I was nervous. About being with Briar, about the familiarity of calling her Bri. About introducing her to Max. About . . . I didn't know what else. Just being here in a new way, perhaps.

I didn't announce my arrival at Orange Julius in the way I normally might, so when Max looked up and saw me—and inexplicably, Bri—about a hundred different questions floated across his face.

First, *What is happening?*

Then, naturally, *Who is she?*

"Yeah, so, this is my friend Max, or Maximillian if you're cool with syllables and such."

"Nobody calls me that. Except, you know. . . ." He pointed at me and smiled. Then he reached across the counter like some kind of fifty-year-old dad and shook Bri's hand.

"So formal," Bri said, and Max blushed. "But nice to meet you, Max."

"How, uh, can I help you? The OrangeBerry Julius is especially good tonight."

This is the smoothest Max has ever been.

"I'll take whatever Jules here is having."

Max gave me this look like he was about to crack up because nobody in my life has ever called me "Jules," and so I gave him one back because when has he ever said something was "especially good tonight"? As expected, I won, and he turned around and started making our Orange Julius Originals without another comment.

"I can't lie. I'm excited," Bri said. "My first Orange Julius."

"You should temper your expectations," I said.

Et tu, Juliana? Et tu?

And then we ran out of things to say, so we looked out into the mall, which was busier than normal. Busy days annoyed me most, when person after person came up to bother Max, stumbling through their drink orders even though we were obviously in the middle of an important conversation. When I could swing it—when Mom was out with Scott or it was summer—I liked to come an hour or so before closing, when the entire mall was slowly powering down and it felt almost illicit to walk through with Max, him showing me all the carefully hidden doors that led to access hallways.

"Okay, here you go," Max said, setting three cups down on the counter.

My breath caught and before I could say anything, Bri pointed at the third cup and said, "You trying to score points with us? Giving us free drinks? I barely know thee, Max."

Max looked completely flustered. He went a deep crimson again and, perhaps out of sheer anxiety, started to say, "I always make two for Julie because—"

"Because I'm a fiend for the Orange," I said.

I didn't know what else to do. It's not like the Man was a secret, not really. But he wasn't not a secret, either. He wasn't something I went volunteering to people I just met—*Hey, would you like to meet my imaginary guardian angel that people let me get away with because my dad died? I know, cool, right?* Bri and Max were both looking at me, so I picked up both cups, double fisting the frozen orange slush and pretending it didn't make me look like a complete psycho.

You just love Orange Julius! You are definitely not a psycho.

Tomato, tomahto, my Man.

"Oh, so you two have, like, a thing," Bri teased.

"No," we both said at the same time, and of course it immediately made it seem like we, in fact, had a thing. I didn't know how to explain that Max and I weren't into the whole "we were friends but now we're dating because we were in love the whole time" trope. We shared something deeper, but that felt too corny to say—especially while holding two large cups of Orange Julius.

"Julie is my best friend," Max said, completely sincere. Bri gave me this look, like, *Oh my God, that's the most darling thing I've ever heard.* And then she turned back to Max with a smile that I knew would melt every part of him, birthing a need to redirect every conversation I would have with him for weeks, months, until he finally convinced himself that he shouldn't ask Bri out.

"Well. Max. I have to say you know how to make a first impression."

"Thank you," Max said, shifting his weight from foot to foot. I could tell he was working up the nerve to say something and I wanted to stop him while he was ahead, before he could drop one of his classic anti-pickup lines. But I was too late and good thing, because somehow he delivered. Like it was his job.

"It's been said before."

This jabroni right here.

Bri laughed, loud and genuine, and Max clearly exploded inside. Fireworks. Mortars. Everything going off like the Fourth of July. I hoped only I could tell. Just before Bri pulled me away, I gave him a look—*Thank you, thank you, thank you.*

Bri and I walked around the mall, stopping to investigate various shops—shops I saw every single day—but the whole vibe was more of a stroll. Eventually I ditched the second Julius because it was melting in my hands and, if Bri noticed, she didn't say anything. When we'd literally made it around every level, including the weird section of the top level that I never visit, with the comedy club and restaurants designed solely for forty-somethings on date nights, and were back in the heart of the mall, I could see Max leaning against the counter, staring at his phone from across the rotunda.

Bri pulled us behind a pillar for cover. She leaned around, shooting a look at Max before hiding again.

"So, seriously. You two aren't a thing?"

"What? Max?" I probably sounded defensive and, as a result, like I was outing myself as secretly in love with Max. I hoped the way I laughed was enough to explain everything.

"Seriously. He's like my brother. I also kind of hate him ninety percent of the time."

She smiled and peered at Max again. "He's cute. And, like, he doesn't know he's cute. Which just makes him cuter."

Max is a good man. A candy-ass jabroni, sure. But a good man.

"I think he secretly practices his pickup lines in the mirror," I said. "Which makes his whole vibe kind of annoying, frankly."

We laughed and Max must've heard us, because he looked up from his phone and immediately straightened. Fixed his shirt and adjusted the dopey hat he wore, scanning the empty rotunda. Just as he was going back to his phone, Bri stepped out from behind the pillar and waved. Max glowed brighter than the fluorescent orange-and-blue Orange Julius sign just above his head. Bri cackled.

"Hey, listen," I said. "I might catch a ride home with Max, if you're cool with that."

Bri was still smiling when she turned to face me. "Oh, sure. Of course. We should eat lunch together again tomorrow. Okay?"

"Uh, yeah. That sounds fun."

Fun!

Okay, okay.

Bri took a step toward the exit but stopped and said, "I had a great time. Like, better than I've had in a while. So, thanks. I needed this."

And then she turned, pausing to give Max a final wave before she walked out the door.

Max had been watching us ever since the wave and must've known I was about to give him the business, so he stopped me before I could start.

"You've been holding out on me. Bri! How do I not know about Bri?"

"Calm down, sparky. Let's not objectify her quite this quickly."

"Yeah, okay. Sorry. It's just . . ."

He stared past me, to the exit. Bri had been gone for a minute, so it was like he was trying to will her back into the space.

"Okay, this is creeping me out," I said.

There's a fine line between captivation and lechery, Max.

"I'm sorry. I'm not trying to be weird. She's just . . . nice."

"And beautiful. Don't forget that."

"Well, yeah. But do you know how many girls come here and treat me like complete shit?"

"I'll fight them."

A suplex in the middle of the ring, Max

"It's just, you get used to being ignored. Or treated like

you don't exist. And I don't know, it feels good for somebody to be decent to me."

I wanted to continue giving him a hard time, say something like *But it's also because she's hot, right?* He was just so terminally earnest. It made me want to grab him into a huge bear hug and never let him go, which probably would have made things weird, so instead I just said, "Well, those other girls don't know what they're missing."

He paused, then nodded. "It's been said before."

CHAPTER FIVE

When I got home, Mom was sitting on the couch with a cup of tea. The television was on, but she wasn't watching it. I sat down next to her and rested my head on her shoulder.

"Do you want a cup?"

"No, I had Orange Julius," I admitted before I could stop myself.

"Good Lord. You realize there isn't a single orange in any of those drinks, right?"

I nodded, ready to crash from the sugar. Ready to let myself forget about the last three years, and just sit here, taking in the smell of Mom's tea, the detergent she's used since I could remember, the vague smell of her office—a mixture of coffee and something that smells almost like cinnamon—still on her clothing, her skin. In a moment like this, I could almost reach how it used to be: Dad stumbling from the kitchen, big and goofy and loud. Unable to move two steps without causing the whole house to shake. "Like a herd of elephants," Mom would say, pretending not to be charmed by every damn thing that man did. It would be sickening if it wasn't so enviable.

What did it mean to have somebody who loves you that way? Not parental love, but the sort of love that was fierce. The sort that didn't have any regard for the wreckage it might leave behind, way before anybody was ready. Before anybody could even say goodbye.

I woke up on the couch, a quilt pulled above my shoulders. The entire house was dark, except for the light above the kitchen sink that was always on. In the distance I could hear the whirring of a fan, a habit Mom picked up from Dad, even though she was always cold. Something about the silence never seemed right, I guess.

When it first happened, we lived in a thick cloud. It wasn't dark, not necessarily, but singularly gray. No way to navigate, nothing to do but stay still. Eventually the cloud lifted and then it was as if we couldn't look directly into the sun. Everything felt too bright, too much, until slowly, we learned to live without Dad the way people always do—by letting the grief become familiar, domestic. At least, that's what we told ourselves. That we were healing. Moving forward. It was the mantra of every grief support group, every weird mixer for people trying to be happy after a loss. You couldn't help but be propelled forward, to solve your grief and mourning on a timeline that society required eventually. But the clouds still came. Sometimes just for a moment. Other times for an entire weekend, the hours spent ordering food in and watching mindless tattoo reality shows on television.

All of this was the great lie of grief, of course. They didn't tell you that in all those groups. People talked about death and loss as something sad. But *sad* could never completely describe the feeling. It was too temporary, as if what we were feeling could fly away in the night or be cured with a sunny day.

No, we were bereft. We had lost a fundamental piece. Something that couldn't be replaced, no matter how much we tried or how hard we wished. It was like floating in empty space. An endless hole, an endless feeling, and—if I were one to be dramatic—an endless sadness that I wasn't sure I even wanted to escape. Because what if escaping meant, to some degree, forgetting? And while I wouldn't say we'd never be happy again—that would be too fatalistic and, weirdly, a little too sentimental—I wasn't sure I believed there was any fixing whatever this was, whatever we'd become.

And here's the thing: what if that wasn't wrong?

What if you shouldn't be ever be okay with losing something fundamental?

I jumped awake.

Mom was in the kitchen, and whether it was the slanting light or some kind of internal clock, I immediately knew I was late.

"You're fine," Mom said when I launched myself off the couch. "Out like a light, though. I tried to wake you up five times. I already called the school and told them you were running a little late."

Late? The Man is never late. He only arrives on time!

I tried to start my morning routine, but something had downshifted in my body and every step was heavier than the last. When Mom found me in my bedroom, face down and essentially moaning on my bed, I didn't know how much time had passed or how I even got under my covers. But I wasn't moving.

"Hey, what's up?"

"I think I'm just down," I said.

"Want me to call in to work? We can make fun of the infomercials and then pretend we don't enjoy the soap operas."

Or we could watch Adrenaline.

"I'm fine. I just want to stay home. You can go to work."

I could feel the look of deep concern, as if she stared long and hard enough, she'd be able to see inside me and find out what was happening.

"Really, Mom, I just didn't sleep well. I'll stay in bed all day and will be fine."

It convinced her enough to come over, tuck me in a little tighter, and give me a gentle kiss on my forehead. The last thing I remembered before I drifted off again was her calling out my name, the door closing, and then the silence of an empty house.

The first email came from Wentz minutes after his class would have started.

??????????????????????

It was surprising how ominous a string of punctuation could be over email, especially compared to Wentz's normal, pleasant way of speaking. I sent him a one-word response—"sick"—and then I didn't hear back from him, which was both satisfying and ultimately what got me out of bed to attempt even basic research for my project, which included watching no less than four episodes of Adrenaline to look for examples of kayfabe in modern wrestling.

You are a research maven, dear.

Max always knew the storylines before they developed, who was turning heel before they surprised the crowd or who was about to pop through the curtain at the last second. Who had contract disputes and whether the marriage on the screen had consequences for a relationship off it. Everything was available online. But it wasn't always that way. At some point, kayfabe mattered. The illusion mattered. Maybe people needed to believe in good versus evil before in a way they no longer do now. Needed to believe that the heels were actual tough customers who wouldn't think twice about knocking you out with a metal chair and, while you were sprawled out on the ground, taking your girl out for a night out on the town just for good measure.

My dad believed.

Or at least, he bemoaned all the ways modern fandom had "ruined wrestling." Even still, sometimes—sometimes—wrestling managed to pull off the stranger-than-fiction trick, where what was happening in the ring was undeniably scripted but somehow seemed more real than our lives—or perhaps, spoke to our lives in a way that nothing else could.

Kayfabe, jabronis.

When I got tired, I searched "never break kayfabe" T-shirts on my phone, wondering whether I could get one here by tomorrow. Soon enough I was so bored I was ready to go running to school to escape. Instead, I sent a text to Max, who hated it when I texted him at school because he was, like, fifty years old and was worried about his future.

Max ditch school and come to my house

Read 10:22 PM

I waited for the three dots to appear. At this point I'd take any message—even one telling me to go to hell, or however he would put it. When nothing appeared, I fired off another text.

If you leave me on read I will never let you make me another orange julius

I, however, will not hold it against you, fine sir.

I gave him a minute, then another one, and then I cursed his name and committed to never sending him another text, ever. Still, I peeked at my phone one last time, but Max had gone dark—silenced his notifications.

We will make him pay. Later. When we go get Orange Julius.

I leaned back in bed. Every time I looked at my phone, I expected it to be ten, fifteen minutes later but barely a minute or two had passed. The talk shows weren't even on television yet, just news. I settled on my pillow, and the frustration gradually transformed into undeniable comfort, pulling me slowly into a dream where I was trying to rescue my childhood dog from, maybe, aliens? And I slept, the dreams growing more and more bizarre, until my phone woke me up.

"What? Hello?"

I was still asleep, but through the fog I heard a voice ask how I was doing. If I had any symptoms. I looked at the clock on my phone—nearly noon.

"What? No. Who is this? How did you get this number?"

Same voice, more fog—the paranoia was thick. But then I heard the word "prom" and something snapped to life.

"Bri?"

"Uh, yeah?"

"This is Bri?"

"Seriously, are you okay?" Bri chuckled nervously on the other line. "I thought it might be the *two* Orange Juliuses last night."

Heresy.

"I only drank one of them. And no, I'm fine."

On the other end, I heard a voice—something about me having an iron stomach.

"Is that Max?"

Bri chuckled and said something I couldn't make out. To Max? Was he just passing by or had he momentarily broken through space and time, a cellular miracle? But that suddenly isn't the story of the day. I needed details.

"You're with Max right now?"

This time she said, "Here," and then I heard Max chuckling—nervous and tight. I could imagine him, shifting his weight from foot to foot as he took the phone from her. Probably trying not to blush as Bri watched him.

"Hey." His voice changed to a whisper. "Bri and I ate lunch together."

Max!

"But seriously—are you . . . you know, okay?" Max asked.

Max knew. I wouldn't have to explain it to him. I could let silence answer his question. You couldn't really explain the tidal wave knocking you from your feet, anyway. It was nothing but the sudden swirl, the pull, disappearing into the deep.

"I just needed a day," I said.

There was a slight tussle—that was the only way I could describe it—and I heard both Bri and Max laughing.

"Okay, we're coming over," she said.

We can all watch Adrenaline. It will be glorious.

"Uh, okay? And Max is . . . coming?"

Max was certainly not coming. I could already hear him hemming and hawing. Bri said something. Then Max. Then Bri again. I have no idea how it resolved, but Bri was back on the phone, chipper as always.

"Great. We'll be there soon."

She hung up. I paused, just long enough to take it in. Then I jumped up and started running around the house, making things presentable and checking my clothes in the mirror, which is ridiculous because who was Bri? What did I care? Max might as well have lived here for the need to put on any airs for him. Though what was alarming was the ease with which Bri invited herself over to my house like some kind of true-crime podcast psycho. At least Max would be with her. Surely we could both take her, if needed.

The doorbell rang.

You and Max can definitely take her, Juliana.

The doorbell rang again, followed by a knock.

The big boot. An atomic drop. One-two-three, out!

I ran down the stairs and opened the door, just enough so I could see Bri, who was alone—dammit, Max, you old man—smiling big. Like a complete psycho. And here I was, a big nasty rain cloud about to shock her with some serious lightning.

"You're not a psycho, right?"

Subtle.

"What?"

"Like, you coming over here. This isn't some kind of psycho thing where you go around and make friends with people and wait until they call in sick to school and then show up at their house to kill them? Plus, where's Max?"

Bri bit her lip, like she was thinking really hard about what to say next about having clearly killed Max and being here to finish me off, too.

"You've really put a lot of thought into this."

Your logic, however, is dazzling!

"I'm sorry. It's just. This doesn't, you know, happen a lot."

"What? People coming to your house?"

"Yeah. And, like, in the middle of the school day. Especially when I just kind of met them yesterday."

Bri nodded. "But wouldn't I have taken care of business when I had you alone in my car?"

This is a true battle of wits.

I had to concede the point, opening the door a little wider—but not too wide.

"Okay, I'm sorry," Bri said, her tone and body language changing immediately. "I do this. Like, I get an idea, *Hey, that would be fun!* But then it, you know, turns out to be creepy and I just wanted to make sure you were okay and Max was talking about how he's had perfect attendance since grade school and how you were fine and . . ."

She shrugged apologetically.

"Seriously, though. I can go."

Juliana, I think she comes as a friend.

Bri walked around, peering into corners and opening doors, going through nearly the whole house before finally joining me in the living room.

"I didn't go in your parents' room," she said before flopping down on the couch. She picked up a magazine Mom had left on the coffee table, flipping through the pages absently before she said, "Yeah, sorry. I'm kind of fully ignoring how weird I'm being."

"Not as much weird," I said. "As, you know, psychotic."

She feigned shock and it made us both laugh.

"Harsh but fair," she said.

"I mean, it's cool. All I had planned was spiraling out of control and possibly eating an entire box of pierogies.

Or what I like to call 'Tuesday.'"

"Well, one out of two ain't bad. Let's fire up the oven!"

I went to the basement to get the box, which was more the size of a crate, from the freezer. Mom, planning ahead. Perhaps even for this day when she knew I would need to eat pan after pan of frozen pierogies. Catharsis in dough and potato form. Or maybe they'd been on sale, an impulse buy from one of her marathon trips to Costco. When I appeared at the top of the stairs, suitcase of pierogies in my hands, Bri jumped with excitement.

"Oh dang, Julie. Your family knows how to party."

It has been said before.

I dropped the box on the table and Bri used her keys to cut through the taped top. As she did, I pulled out two pans—two pans should be enough—and hit them with the cooking spray. Bri already had a handful of frozen pierogies in her hand and arranged them on the first pan. Both pans were in the oven before we said another word.

"That was some damn teamwork," Bri said. "I'm low-key impressed with how we knocked that out."

I laughed. "One time in sixth grade Max and I were trying to make brownies or something and I was staring at the box and thinking, There's no way this is only three ingredients."

"Oh no. I already see where this is going," Bri said, turning around one of our kitchen table chairs and sitting in it.

"And yeah, so I'm thinking, it needs something."

It ain't flour!

"I'd seen my mom bake and she always used flour. . . ."

I could still see Max's face when we pulled the monstrosity out of the oven, climbing out of the pan like we'd somehow created life. It was everywhere, burned to the racks of the stove. Smelling like hell itself.

"You totally took a bite, didn't you?"

I nodded, laughing. "We had to at least try it. What if we'd accidentally stumbled onto something revolutionary?"

Bri shook her head and chuckled. "Speaking of Max. Let us not forget that he has disappointed us."

"He was already on my list for not texting me back."

"He really is an old man," Bri said.

"One hundred percent. And not only did he leave me on read, but he also turned off his notifications."

She sat upright. "Retribution shall be swift. And appropriate. Come over here."

I wasn't sure why she started running her fingers through her hair, making it messy, but when she started to do it to me, too, I nearly jumped out of my own skin.

"Trust me," she said, grabbing my cell phone and getting ready to take a selfie. "Get in close. Look sexy."

She took a pic. We looked ridiculous.

"I said 'sexy'! Not 'I just woke up and sucked on a lemon'!"

I had no idea how to look sexy and I had no desire to figure it out right then. Bri, however, was moving the phone up and down, left and right, searching for the perfect angle—an obvious pro. Before I could say anything else, she snapped five pictures fast and then paused to inspect them.

"Oh hell, yes. You look amazing in this one. And so do I; I'm not going to lie."

I looked and what she had done with a combination of lighting, camera angle, and catching me right before I yelled, "I look ridiculous!" was nothing short of miraculous.

"And noooowwwww," Bri sang out the words of her sentence as she typed on my phone, smiling when the *whoosh* of the text message was sent. "He will text you back."

"What did you do," I said.

"Trust me," Bri said. "Max is sitting in, like, trig right now and we just blew his mind. He could've texted you back. He could've left with me and been here for all *this*."

She performed a comically provocative shimmy that made both of us laugh our asses off, just as my phone pinged—a new message.

Bri picked up the phone and raised her eyebrows as she showed me the message.

what

Before I could say anything, another message.

how

A third.

I can't . . . what!

The oven dinged.

CHAPTER SIX

We were eating pierogies right off the baking sheet when Mom walked through the door, humming a song to herself. She came up the stairs and saw Bri first, dropping the mail and yelling out before I could stop her.

"Mom, it's okay—this is Bri, she's a . . . friend. From school."

Not a psycho.

Bri stood up and held out her hand to shake, but Mom was still trying to process. Bri pulled her hand back and said, "Yeah, so, I heard Julie was sick, and I decided to skip school and come over to keep her company."

When Mom still didn't respond, Bri turned to me and whispered, "Okay, you're right. This sounds completely psychotic."

Mom gave me a look like, *Who is this person?* and I tried to return one that said, *You wouldn't believe me even if I told you.* Thankfully, it only took Mom a beat to go from Stranger Danger to Chipper Hostess—her normal operating mode. She grabbed a pierogi and sat down at the table with us.

"Well, thank God for good friends," she said, giving me a wink.

Bri, unlike that jabroni Max, is good people.

Mom picked up a second pierogi, but before she put it in her mouth, she said, "Oh, I just got off the phone with Mr. Wentz and—"

I groaned loudly, perhaps a bit dramatically. Enough that both Mom and Bri gave me a look and then shared their own, something like, *Can you believe the drama happening at this table right now?*

"You like Mr. Wentz," Mom said.

"Everybody likes Mr. Wentz," Bri confirmed.

"Yeah, he's fine. Teacher of the year, all that. But he totally sabotaged me into this whole prom committee."

"Hey! What's wrong with the prom committee?!" Bri sat upright, indignant with her smile.

"Uh, nothing . . . ," I said, grabbing a pierogi and cramming it into my mouth. "But I guess I would've liked to have had some agency in the decision."

"'It will be good for you.' That's what Mr. Wentz said—he's just so helpful."

"Oh yeah," Bri said. She cleared her throat, and then nailed a pitch-perfect Wentz impersonation. "Uh, Julie, the important thing isn't what I think you should do with your education, but what *you* do with your education."

I laughed so hard, I almost knocked one of the baking sheets off the table. Mom caught the pan before we lost the pierogies. She barely knew Wentz, so she couldn't appreciate how uncanny the impersonation was. All she cared about was whether I was falling behind—normal parent stuff.

"Well-done," I mumbled, and Bri gave me a quick bow.

"He just wants to make sure you are . . ." Mom glanced at Bri, trying to offer me the protection of vagueness. "Connected. You know."

"Connected?" Bri asked.

"Dead dad," I said. "Very sad."

There was a beat, like all the oxygen had been sucked from the room. Bri nodded once. Then a second time. Mom looked at me and then Bri, trying to decide if she should be worried or embarrassed.

"Well, that sounds hard," Bri said. "I'm really sorry."

"It's been a few years now," Mom said. "But we're doing okay. Right, honey?"

Normally, I would deflect. Wasn't healing subjective by definition?

"Yeah, I think so," I said. "It makes me think of kayfabe."

"Oh Lord," Mom said.

"Kay who? Does she go to Central?"

Mom chuckled to herself, closing her eyes for a second. Because even though she didn't want to know about kayfabe. . . she knew about kayfabe. When she opened them and looked at me, I could see it. The loss. The grief, which she hides so easily now. All of it probably wrapped around the first time Dad had told her about kayfabe in some dingy pizza joint, huddled over a pizza in a back corner booth. Him wild-eyed with excitement, her trying to keep up. Both madly in love.

"It's not a 'who,'" I told Bri. "It's a 'what.'"

A way of life.

When I looked back at Mom, whatever grief had creeped into her head was slowly slipping back away. She could see it in my smile, perhaps hear it in the excitement in my voice. At least right now, I was okay.

"It makes you ask, are we pretending we're okay or are we really okay? Or, now that I think about it, if we are pretending to be okay, does that mean we really are okay?" I said. "Really makes you think. Kayfabe."

"Oh. Well. That explains . . . everything," Bri said.

Well, of course it does!

Mom rubbed my shoulder and stood up, picking up a last pierogi and saying, "Well, as much as I would like to dive deep into kayfabe, I need to get ready. Hot date." I cringed and she laughed. Before she left the kitchen, she stopped and said, "I'm glad to meet you, Bri. Especially if you can keep this one from having Orange Julius for dinner."

She popped the last bite of pierogi into her mouth and then walked back to her bedroom. It wasn't a minute later that the doorbell rang, and I assumed it was Scott because it was always Scott. So, I ran down the stairs and opened the door without a second thought.

When Max tumbled into my house, looking around like a kid on Christmas morning, I was momentarily surprised. Bri didn't miss a beat.

"Oh, *now* he shows up."

* * *

I told Mom we were going to the Mall and she yelled for us to be safe as we went out the door. Max, in his fervor—he did not like me using this word, which made me want to use it all the more—had skipped the whole stop-at-home part of his after-school routine and now was sitting in the back of Bri's car, changing into his Orange Julius shirt and swearing up and down that he had rushed to my house because he was worried about me.

"You never know!"

Oh, Max, my dear boy.

"What! I'm not lying!"

Bri and I were officially dead now, cold and six feet under, nodding very seriously, which only made Max more indignant.

"But really, what did you all do this afternoon while I was at school?"

Bri looked at me, then at the rearview mirror, raising her eyebrows—a straight killer. I didn't want to think about whatever stupid fiction had been playing in his head, let alone have him articulate it for us. So, in a moment of weakness, I granted him a reprieve.

"We made pierogies. We talked about kayfabe. We sent you that text message."

Max's eyes narrowed as he searched my face for any hint of a lie.

"Jesus, Max What do you think was happening? Like, pillow fights in our underwear and—I don't know—experimenting?"

Max went a shade of red I didn't know existed, a new entry for the color wheel. He pulled his Orange Julius hat down a little lower over his eyes before saying, "Well, no. Of course not. Stop making stuff weird. Jesus, Julie."

This cracked Bri like an egg. Soon enough, I was laughing, too. Max, however, was holding strong—still deep in his embarrassment, his paranoia.

His fervor.

Yes, fervor!

When we pulled up to the entrance to the Mall, Bri hit the power locks so Max couldn't get out. Which I would probably have to mention to her later because who did this, except psychos?

"Maximillian," Bri said, glancing at me for approval. I slow clapped. Well-done.

"Jeez, not you, too."

"We request your presence after the shift selling your wares."

"I don't have wares. God."

Bri was undeterred. She nudged me and I sat up a little straighter and made eye contact with Max.

"Don't be that way, Maximillian. We are your friends."

That is right, Maximillian.

"Today, after your shift, we will return," Bri continued. "Upon that time, we will expect two Orange Juliuses."

Ahem.

Max gave me a look with a small smile. Bri tapped the steering wheel before pointing to her eyes, then to Max's.

"Two Orange Juliuses! And then you will accompany us to a destination of our choosing! Perhaps bowling! I know a spot!"

"Shouldn't that be 'knoweth a spot,'" Max deadpanned, and Bri, just as quickly, unlocked the car door. Not without a smile, I noticed.

"You tire me. You are released. Just be ready."

Max got out of the car, happy with the point he'd obviously scored. Bri waited until she was sure he was no longer in earshot, and she looked at me and grinned.

"He really is cute as hell."

Bri told me we weren't going home, that we were on a pilgrimage—which seemed a bit much, if I'm being honest—until Max was off work and then we would go bowling. She had unilaterally decided that was the plan for the night.

"There's this place, across the river, which sounds kind of sketchy—and it's kind of in this weird industrial area—but totally safe! Anyway, it's a bowling alley. I used to go there a lot and I'm supposed to be, like, reclaiming stuff I used to do. It's a whole therapy thing."

It was the last thing Bri said for a long time.

We drove around Minneapolis, crossing over into St. Paul, and then back into Minneapolis at a different spot on the river. The daylight was dying all around us. A liminal moment, a thin place, right before the streetlights turned on—making the world seem darker than it actually was.

At a stoplight, Bri started a new playlist and turned

up the radio—new life in her face, her body. I'd never heard the song before—it outed itself as Christian music almost immediately—starting off with drums, then slowly becoming this wannabe epic song about how the singer was bad but wanted to be good and then there were about five thousand different choruses to that effect—if only he could love God the way God loved him, all that.

Jesus-is-my-boyfriend music.

I laughed and immediately felt bad.

"Sorry. I used to be really into this stuff," Bri said. I could see her smile in the faint light of the dashboard. "I know it's terrible."

"No, I'm enjoying it," I lied.

"You're the worst liar I've ever met," Bri said, laughing. "But thank you for being nice."

"I mean, okay. It's kind of terrible. But hey, like, I can talk. If you hadn't come over I would've probably spent my day watching professional wrestling videos and calling it research."

Bri took a minute to process this information. At this point, I was used to it. And I fully expected her next question to be where she could drop me off—that, oh shucks, the bowling alley was closed tonight. Not that the fiftieth verse of "Will You Marry Me, Jesus?" wasn't grounds for a quick exit, too.

Instead, she looked at me seriously and said, "I think neither of us should speak about this playlist or professional wrestling ever again."

How dare you.

We didn't talk again for a long time, each song in Bri's playlist getting more sentimental—more religious—than the last. It was certainly weird and transcended good taste, but more surprisingly it violated one of the great rules of adolescence: never let people peek behind the curtain. Never let them see your weirdness. Be cool, at all costs.

And that, of course, became the rub. Never let them know the angle, the story—the real you. If nobody knows you, you won't get hurt. You won't spend years climbing up a sand dune of grief and loss, sliding back down every step.

The last time I met with my therapist—it had been months now—she asked me if I thought turning inward, assuming that nobody else could understand what I was going through, was healthy. I wanted to believe that nobody could understand the individual pain of losing Dad, the coals of grief being pressed against my tongue every single day. Dad, who believed to the very end that kayfabe existed, and commonly told us if the wackos could follow Sky Daddy, then he could believe in this.

The counselors and therapists told me grief was universal—maybe the only universal thing—but sometimes I'd spend entire nights thinking and worrying, because if we're all hiding and we're all navigating the complex formula of who we can let in, who we can trust with the sad, the happy, even the bizarre parts of ourselves, does that mean we always end up alone?

No, dear.

Bri slowed to a stop at a red light and glanced at me, her eyes momentarily flashing with the passing headlights of another car. I rubbed my eyes and said, "I'm guessing you don't pop this on at a party."

Bri chuckled. "Back in middle school, this was the party playlist, Julie."

Christians! At a party.

"That's . . . interesting."

Bri shot me a look and then drummed her hands on the steering wheel. "Anyway, okay! Emo Bri was engaged for a moment and I'm sorry you had to see that. But I'm back? Yay?"

She did some jazz hands and quickly put them back on the wheel as we started moving forward through the changed light.

I took a chance and said, "So tell me more about lunch with Max."

She lit up like Christmas. "Oh, he was so nervous. Like, he barely talked at first."

"That tracks," I said.

"But once he got past being completely mystified that I not only remembered him but was sitting there waiting for him. Well, you. But I let him believe. Hope eternal, all that. Once he got past all that? He was really great. And sweet. And hilarious."

"Please calm down," I said, chuckling.

Bri and Max at lunch. It made him not skipping school

even more impressive, as he was surely sweating every interaction, every word they shared.

"I guarantee that made his year," I said.

"Well, it was fun. I still only have a few friends at Central. And they're from our church youth group. . . ." She sighed. "Anyway, it's complicated. As they say."

"Complicated . . . sucks."

"Complicated does suck," she said.

We were almost to the Mall of America's entrance and Bri switched the music to a less Jesus-centric playlist. She wove through the lot, navigating back to the door where we'd dropped off Max. He was leaning against the wall—three cups of Orange Julius in his hand.

Good man.

Bri ran her hands through her hair and blew air through her lips before she honked the horn. Max ran to get in the back seat of the car. He handed me and then Bri a cup, smiling as he put the third one next to him on the back seat.

"Okay. Let's do this," Bri said.

CHAPTER SEVEN

When we pulled up to the bowling alley, I laughed.

"It's called Memory Lanes," I said.

"Yeah? You've been here before?"

"Memory lanes. It's a pun, Bri."

She looked puzzled. Then it clicked.

"Oh! I've been coming here my whole life and I never got that before!"

As we walked across the parking lot, Max began listing all other possible bowling puns—many of them not appropriate for a respectable, family-owned bowling joint with a large neon sign in the parking lot.

"Bowl Movements," however, is the one that made Bri pause just inside the doors and face him. She put a hand on his chest and I watched him evaporate into nothing.

"Please. I'm begging you to stop."

Max nodded and held up a single finger and quickly said, "Dry Bumpers. I'm so sorry, but I had to."

Bri's eyes went wide, and she slapped him on the chest. She laughed all the way to the counter, where a rather bored-looking college kid was working. Before any of us could give him our sizes, somebody yelled out my name.

"Jules!"

Jules. I think this might be the start of a trend, Juliana.

Uh, no, and besides, the place was packed, so I wasn't sure they were even talking to me. But then I saw Scott, his teeth, every part of him shining brighter than the neon outside. He was wearing a bowling shirt, because of course he was, and five different bracelets worked down his arm like slots in a machine as he waved. He pulled Mom to her feet. He pointed, double finger guns to the group. He was coming right for us.

"Oh my dear God," Max whispered to me. "Is that . . . Scott?"

Yes. Yes it is, my boy.

Max knew about Scott, of course, and Greg and Kathy knew Mom had started to date again. But none of them had yet experienced Scott, who danced through the crowd, his smile like a lighthouse guiding the way. Mom stayed behind, typing their names into the screen mounted to the ceiling.

"Jules!" He went for the hug, and I wanted to stop him like, whoa there, that's not who we are, my guy, but I let it happen and it was over soon enough.

Jules. This jabroni right here.

"What are you doing here?" he asked. "And who are these two?"

"Uh, bowling?" I said, which came across grumpier than

I intended, so I made a U-turn, if only for Mom's sake. "And this is Max. And Bri."

Nobody had ever been happier to meet two random strangers than Scott was in that exact moment. He went in for a hug on Max, who took a step back but still got swept away. Bri moved behind me to avoid the coming embrace, put her hands in a praying position which, honestly, might've made Scott even happier.

"Max! So good to finally meet you! And Bri! Yeah! Namaste!"

Scott took it all in. Hands on hips. All those teeth.

"Why don't you all come bowl with us—it's on me." Bri and Max looked at me, as if it was my decision. Maybe hoping I'd stomp my foot or hit Scott with the ennui. But Scott brought out the big gun. Guilt.

"Your mom would love it, Jules."

Jules!

"Yeah, okay. Maybe a game or two."

Scott clapped his hands and turned to the college student at the counter.

"Okay, Peter, we're going to need three more pairs of shoes—you all, give him your sizes—and let's go ahead and reserve the lane next to ours. Cool?"

Peter grunted and typed something into his computer before getting our sizes and our shoes. Scott, to his credit, seemed to be loving every minute of this. By the time we had our shoes on, he was back with two pitchers of pop, a promise of nachos, fries, and pizza—even a stack of quarters.

"For the video games. In case you get bored with us olds."

The gesture practically made Mom fall off the chair, but luckily, she was able to fall into Scott instead. It was as if she just needed to touch him, and he'd given her the opening. I watched, unsure what I was feeling.

New love. Gross.

Bowling started out about as awkward as you'd expect, with Scott trying too hard and us acting too cool. But then Bri got a strike, followed by another, and when the third crashed down, Scott jumped to his feet yelling, "Turkey! Turkey! Turkey!"

Every single one of us was, like, What is happening right now?

But then Peter came loping over to the lane, dragging a comically huge stuffed turkey that he grudgingly placed on one of the empty chairs.

"We celebrate your accomplishment," he said with the affect of a dead tuna, before trudging back to the counter.

"Uh, what just happened?" Max said.

"Three strikes in a row," Mom said. "Scott has taught me a lot."

"Yeah! Next strike is a domestic turkey. Six in a row, wild turkey. Golden turkey is nine. And, naturally, a dinosaur is a perfect game."

"Naturally," Bri whispered to me, and I had to cough to keep from laughing.

Not that Scott would have noticed, because he was fully

into it now, practically lecturing on the history of bowling and its working-class origins. How the food names, like *turkey*, were once actual edible prizes, and not stuffed monstrosities that leered at you like they knew all your secrets.

"That thing is creeping me out," I said, laughing. Max stood up and put his Orange Julius hat on the turkey's head, covering his felted eyes.

"Oh gross, you don't know where that thing's been," Bri said, covering her own eyes for some reason. Max slid next to her and poked her once in the side, laughing when she jumped—as if the cooties of the turkey monster somehow hopped seats.

"Jerk," she said, but it had all the bite of a sugar cookie.

I, meanwhile, couldn't hit a pin if Jesus himself came back and directed the ball down the lane. Not with Scott's expert advice or Mom's unfailing encouragement. A big fat zero on the scoreboard.

Bowling is overrated, Juliana. However, I do love yelling out, "Turkey!"

Bri didn't get another strike, which dampened the mood a bit because I was pretty invested in what might appear in our lane if one of us were to yell out, "Domestic turkey!"

"Domestic Turkey should be my new nickname," Max said. "I think I could pull that off."

"I swear to God, if you say it again, I will never refer to you as anything but 'Domestic Turkey,'" I said, and he leaned all of his weight into me until I stood up for my turn, nearly making him fall.

In a moment of what can only be described as inspiration, I yelled out, "Domestic Turkey!" when I threw my ball. A slight breach of etiquette, but it worked.

The ball was true, the line straight. Ten pins, crashing down. Thank you, Baby Jesus.

"Domestic Turkey! Domestic Turkey! Domestic Turkey!" Bri yelled, laughing wildly. Behind her, Peter squinted at our screen, shaking his head after confirming that no domestic turkey had been achieved. At first Scott seemed a bit put off by our lack of respect for the historical nuances of the game, but eventually he laughed and went to talk to Peter. Kids these days, you know.

Max grabbed the stack of quarters. "Domestic Turkey is about to go dominate some technology."

Max, this is not the way.

Bri rolled her eyes, but I could already see the beginnings of a connection between the two. Only thin tendrils now, but they would grow stronger if they were handled correctly. It made sense. Max was the kind of guy you didn't expect to meet and when you did, he almost seemed impossible. He was, for lack of a better word, *nice.* Which, in the pool of high school boys, made him a unicorn. So when Bri followed him to the machines, I stayed put.

I caught Mom watching Scott at the counter, smiling as he worked his yoga sunshine magic on Peter. Something inside me softened, pushing me to acknowledge the moment. She was changing. And this was important.

"I'm having fun," I said.

She turned, tired but happy. For a second I worried about how tired she looked. How much life had drained from her. She patted me on the leg once.

"I can't believe you yelled 'domestic turkey,' Julie."

"It worked, didn't it?"

"You are so much like your father," she said. "He wouldn't be caught dead in a bowling alley, but I see him in you. The way you walk. Everything."

I didn't know what to say.

Say "thank you," Juliana.

"What did he have against bowling? I mean, I totally blame him for never taking me and, hence, my lack of skill. But bowling? Was it some sort of ethical thing?"

Mom snorted, covering her mouth. She leaned close, as if he was sitting right next to us—as if he could hear.

"He was terrible. We went on a date, and I destroyed him, and I guess even your father had moments of, let's say, thinness when it came to his ego."

Mom laughed. And God, I wished he were here right now. I wished we could rib him and force him into a bowling league. To have him close again, to smell him. To feel him. To lean against his broad shoulders and know that he would never let me fall.

"I'm happy you all showed up here tonight."

I didn't even have to lie when I said, "Me, too."

I looked around. The crowd, the music, the feeling that, decades later, this place was still best designed for smoke-filled nights, pitchers of beer, and the sort of connections currently happening over by the claw machine, where Bri was seesawing between laughter and playful mockery. Even from here, I could see how hard Max was working to win her something, to win her over. Bri's excitement was just as evident, a bright, strobing light engulfing the small arcade.

"They're cute," Mom said.

"Yeah, it's disgusting. And it's only going to get worse."

"Is that . . . a problem? Her and Max?"

"No," I said, rolling my eyes. "Max is . . . not that. At least, for me."

"Okay," Mom said, leaning back in her chair. "Just making sure."

"How about you and Scott? How's your heart chakra?"

Mom demurred at first, but I caught her looking over at Scott again, who was now showing his mandala tattoo to Peter. While it wasn't as feverish as Max and Bri, she couldn't pull her eyes away from him as she spoke.

"He's . . . different, you know?"

You can say that again, amirite, Juliana?!

"I think he's, like, kind of everything coming full circle for me," Mom said. Then she shot me a sideways look. "And let me tell you, he looks good in yoga shorts."

"Jesus, Mom. Too much information."

She shrugged and I didn't want to look at her, to catch a vague lust cross her eyes. To live in fear of hearing a muffled moan, a creak from her room—and I couldn't go any further because, no.

No.

"Well, it's true. What do you want me to do, lie to you?"

"Yes. Please. Lie. To. Me."

We both fell into laughter just as Scott was walking up. He looked confused, but it didn't lower the wattage of his smile.

Let us change the subject, jabroni.

"Hey, Jules, what about a ride home?" Scott rubbed Mom's shoulder as he talked to me. Once again, never "Jules," I wanted to say, but I shook my head and pointed over to Bri and Max, still struggling with the claw machine.

"No, I need to play chaperone for those two."

Scott whispered something in Mom's ear and they both giggled—giggled!—and so when Scott reached into his pocket and pulled out another fistful of quarters, I grabbed them and practically sprinted to Max and Bri.

As I reached them, Max was holding his last quarter up to the sky, as if asking for God's blessing. He blew on it, rubbed it between his hands, and kissed it before dropping it into the slot with a long exhale.

"You got this," Bri said to him.

She turned to me, shook her head, and mouthed, "He doesn't. . . ."

"I can totally see you!" Max said. "Why would you do that? I can totally see you!"

"We're rooting you on, Maximillian," I said. "Don't ruin your luck!"

He breathed deeply again, whispered a prayer to whatever God handled vending machines and arcade games, and lowered the claw. When it came up empty, he cussed loudly.

"I don't know why I'm doing this. I don't even believe in these bullshit mating rituals."

"Mating rituals?" Bri and I said together.

Mating ritual. Oh, Max.

He turned around, red as hell and frustrated. "You know what I mean! I'm a feminist, okay!"

I pushed past Bri and dropped a quarter into the slot. Two seconds later she was holding a stuffed cheetah and Max had gone mute. Which was fine. I had enough words for all of us.

"It might be regressive," I said. "But I kind of like mating rituals."

"It does make things simple," Bri said. "You know, for us ladies."

"I hate both of you," Max said, rubbing his temples. "I really, really do."

I dropped another quarter into the slot, this time pulling out a rather ridiculous-looking octopus. Bri screamed, reaching down and grabbing it out of the bin at the bottom of the machine. Max started walking away, not stopping even when Bri yelled out his name. At first I thought he was made of steel because he just dropped his shoes off at the counter with Peter and kept walking toward the front door. Bri glanced at me. But then he did an about-face and yelled above the din of the bowling alley.

"I need you to respect my privacy in this time of despair."

When he walked out of the bowling alley, Bri grinned.

"I totally own him."

"It's really kind of embarrassing for him," I said.

And then for whatever reason, I suddenly didn't want to keep on joking. Maybe it was the way Max looked—happy, so damn happy—even as we were giving him shit. But I didn't know what to say without sounding ridiculous.

"You okay?" Bri said, bumping my shoulder. "You want the octopus?"

"No. It's just . . . nothing. It's nothing."

She handed me the octopus anyway and I wrapped his tiny tentacles around my hand.

"We should probably go out there and make nice with Max," she said. But she didn't move toward the shoe counter. "Hey, thanks for doing this with me. This place is . . . I don't know, special? Or it used to be. It was nice to be here, having fun, and distracted from, you know, everything."

Something changed on Bri's face. Maybe it was just the dim lights of the bowling alley, or a new trick of the arcade lights, but she suddenly looked sad. But that wasn't the right word, was it? Instead, it was the look of a person who had lost something. A haunted, hollowed-out look that grabbed you with icy hands when you least expected them.

"Anytime. Seriously."

This was a good night, Juliana.

CHAPTER EIGHT

The next morning, I was up early and headed to school filled with a strange energy. Maybe it was misplaced concern because Mom hadn't come home before I fell asleep, and I woke up to a text that said she'd left for work early. A digital version of the walk of shame, I guess, because when I went in her room looking for a hairbrush, her bed hadn't been touched.

The Man is speechless.

It's gross, but it wasn't affecting me because after we left the bowling alley, we just drove around. The windows down, a different playlist. A soft murmur beneath the wind. I was in the back seat, but I could see Max's and Bri's hands creeping closer, closer, closer, until they finally touched. It felt like something that needed to be celebrated. When Max got out of the car, he practically floated to his front door. Even Bri seemed a bit ruffled by the hand-on-hand action, stumbling over her words as she said goodbye to me.

I couldn't remember the last time I was able to let go completely, to forget. The last time I slept as soundly as I had last night. As soon as the thought crossed my mind, I felt the stab of guilt. The familiar pain of forgetting.

Forgetting and healing are two different things, Juliana.

Of course, all that changed as soon as I walked into Central, because I half expected Wentz to appear wanting my project proposal or a prom committee update or whatever, but when he saw me, he just told me about how he and his husband tried to watch some wrestling documentary but they couldn't because their goldendoodle was being extra cute and then he showed me, like, twenty pictures.

"You seem better," he said.

It felt like a trap, so I gave him a side-eye as I was, like, "I'll take your word for it."

But all he said was "You should!" And then told me he'd see me in class. I was still reeling when I heard my name.

"Julie? That's your name, right?"

It was the two skater boys who'd been trying to help hang the prom banner the other day. The shorter one held his skateboard behind his head but was pointing at me with his other hand. I nodded and was about to go back to my phone when he sat down next to me. Close.

"I figure if, like, we're going to be on the same committee, we should do introductions. Be all congenial. I'm Leg. And this is my friend God."

"Excuse me?" I said. "Leg? God? Are you two high?"

"It's a skateboarding thing," God said. "And I'm not high. Leg? Maybe."

"Yeah, it's possible," Leg said, laughing like he was, well, very high. "And anyway, you've never seen anybody that can do things on a skateboard like my man God."

"And for the record, I'm pretty sure we are not on the prom committee, bro," God said.

"I filled out the paperwork!" Leg said. "That girl can't keep me off the committee just because she's scared of innovation!"

"So, yeah, my guy is really into prom," God said. "Has been since freshman year."

"And your friend Bri thinks I'm a joke. But I'm not."

He went immediately sober, leaning forward on the table and staring me directly in the eyes. It was uncomfortable eye contact, the sort you want to shake. For a second I thought he might cry, which of course made me once again think that he was high.

"Prom matters," he said. "Like, I know it's stupid and I shouldn't care about it—but you only get one chance to do this. They don't have prom in college. Or, like, if you work at Chipotle or something."

"Chipotle," God said. "We should get Chipotle for lunch, bro."

Leg seemed to care deeply about prom, which made the whole situation even more bizarre. We had returned to the serious, intense eye contact—nearing twenty seconds— when God laughed and pulled Leg toward him, "Okay, champ, we need to go to class."

Leg seemed to shake out of his trance and gave me a smile.

"See you at the meeting this afternoon?"

"Yeah. I can't wait," I deadpanned.

I was dying to talk to Bri. I wanted to get the dirt on what I assumed had turned into a late-night texting session with Max. Max wasn't a player. He didn't even know the game. So inevitably the texts had been adorable. Bri was likely already floating down the hallways to what I was now considering our table.

Max doesn't know the game. I lol, Juliana.

I also needed to understand what the deal was with God and Leg. Were they the problem that Wentz wanted me to fix? To go all Masked Man on them? Pick up one of the stray folding chairs from the band room and take care of the problem in the parking lot after school? They seemed nice enough, if completely feral and hopelessly antisocial. But you know . . . cute. So why was Bri threatened by their presence?

Five minutes passed and no Bri.

Ten more, and I started eating my lunch without her.

Max finally showed up, ruffled and breathing hard. At first I thought he was the reason Bri was late. Maybe they were hiding under a staircase somewhere, or behind a closed door.

"Um, what were you doing?"

He gave me a strange look and threw his Spanish book onto the table. *"Tratando de no fallar."*

And because Frau Bau was convinced I was going to be a German scholar or something, committing me to four years on the sheer basis of her belief in me, I had no idea what he was saying. So I used the only Spanish I knew, which admittedly I'd learned from the Grand Mysterio, a masked luchador who was criminally under booked in Adrenaline.

"Que pendejo!"

Max stopped and squinted at me. "You realize what you just said, right?"

"No clue. Something about your mother?"

Max laughed. "Anyway. Where's Bri?"

"I was hoping you'd tell me," I said. "I figured you two were . . ."

I wasn't sure what I was going to say, but trailing off made it seem like I was about to get explicit, which I guess I was. And now Max was looking at me like I was completely off my rocks, so I did the only thing I know how to do in situations like this—a flawless reversal.

"She likes you, by the way," I said. He was already eating his sandwich.

"I know."

I know! This jabroni!

"Oh, you know."

Max took another bite of sandwich and tried to stop himself from smiling. I let him have it because he deserved it and, honestly, I wasn't sure I wanted the details of how he "knew" at this point.

When he finished eating, he said, "We texted back and forth a lot last night."

"Did she seem sad to you?"

"No. I mean, I don't know. Am I supposed to know that?"

Max started to look panicked and so I shook my head. "You probably just kept her up too late."

The problem with making a new friend—and let's just acknowledge how cringey even saying something like that was at this point in my life. What? Was Mom going to write Bri's phone number down and magnet it to the refrigerator? Set up a playdate? Anyway, the problem was neither Max nor I knew anyone Bri knew. I didn't know her social safety nets, the people who could tell me to chill out because she was, like, getting her HPV vaccine, which was way too much information. But I was working from a lack of institutional knowledge. And Max? Well, Max was hopeless. Staring off into the ether of the cafeteria. Okay, now I was probably being a psycho, but I did have her number.

Text her, jabroni!

Sure, I could just text her all casual, definitely not like a psycho, like, What up? Because she literally did it to me yesterday, right? But there was also that weird imposter friend syndrome thing happening. Maybe I'd completely misread our situation. That we weren't that kind of friends, which was ridiculous, but in situations like this, I was pretty good at jettisoning all rational thinking.

I pulled out my phone, because c'mon Julie, get a grip, and I tapped out a quick message.

Had fun last night. Missed you at lunch. Will you be at the prom meeting?

And then I sat there, staring at my phone.

* * *

By the end of the day, I wouldn't say I was panicking but I wasn't what you'd call calm. And let me be absolutely clear: I had no reason to think something was wrong. But when we were alone in her car last night—trick of the light, maybe—had my mind working overtime. I'd been in that small, familiar place so often. The one where I didn't need to cry but I also didn't feel whole. People rarely noticed and reacted even less. It was incredibly lonely. And I couldn't unsee it.

So, I did the only thing I could think to do and hoofed it over to Wentz's room. He was packing his bag and looked surprised to see me, especially when I didn't launch into our typical repartee.

"Did you see Bri today?"

Wentz shook his head. "I'm pretty sure she was out today."

"But we have a prom committee meeting."

"Well, Julie, you can still go to the meeting. There are other committee members. Bri doesn't have to be there for you to attend, right?"

I studied Wentz's face. He wasn't the sort of teacher who would lie to your face in the name of some adult sense of propriety. If anything, he was a little too honest and seemed to relish "keeping it real," as my dad had liked to say.

Real recognizes real, Wentz.

I must've looked like a complete fiend or something because he laughed and said, "I am glad that you and Bri have become friends—that's a good connection."

"I'm being stupid, aren't I?"

"Hey, it's not stupid to care about people. It's kind. It's a good thing. Okay?"

Wentz started walking out the door and then he snapped his fingers and turned around like something had just come to mind. I already knew it was going to be some teacher business so I wasn't surprised when he told me he'd read my project proposal, followed by a full-term, about-to-pop, pregnant pause.

"You turned in a paragraph, Julie."

"It's throat clearing," I said. "The calm before the brilliance."

Wentz didn't blink. "How about a little more? I mean, if it can fit into your busy schedule."

I muttered something like, "You're the worst" and in true Wentz form, he held a hand up to his heart and said, "This means so much to me, Julie. This is why I show up. To mold young minds."

Mold this, Wentz!

"Get to your meeting, Julie—and when you speak of me, speak kindly."

God and Leg were standing in the corner of the room whispering to each other, while Penelope and Margo were both staring at their phones. When the two girls saw me, they rolled their eyes, perhaps hoping that Bri would decide to show up.

"This is a quorum," Leg said. "Let's vote."

"For the hundredth time, we are not changing the theme. Especially not without Bri here," Penelope said. "You joined the committee too late!"

"So, you're saying we're on the committee," Leg said.

"I didn't. And we are not changing the theme at all!" Margo clarified. "We've already printed the banner."

"Well, somebody—I don't know who—stole the banner," Leg said, coughing. "So, we'll, uh, need a new one."

"Somebody," God deadpanned. "Who could it be."

"Anyway, moving on," Leg continued. "Enchanted gardens. What does it mean? Let me answer that for you: nothing. I contend that we vote to change it."

"Uh, do you have another option?" I asked.

Both Margo and Penelope looked up from their phones, as if I were encouraging a toddler to wipe his dinner on the walls.

"What? It's not like we're dealing with Faulkner here?" I said. "If he has a good idea, I'd be willing to hear it."

"Bri is going to be pissed," Margo warned.

"Who cares," Penelope said, looking back at her phone. "But *Top Gun* prom? Absolutely not."

Leg looked flustered for a moment. "Well, when you just say it that way, all flat, it doesn't really have the same, I don't know, pizzazz."

"Top Gun?" I asked.

"With the proper buildup, it really makes sense," Leg said.

"It's his Mona Lisa," God said.

"We are not voting to change the prom theme without Bri," Margo said definitively.

"Well . . . we could, you know, have a vote of—"

"No confidence," God said.

Leg snapped his fingers. "Yes! No Confidence! In the prom theme! And then we'll vote on other, better themes, at the next meeting. Okay, who's ready to vote!"

Nobody raised their hands. Penelope sighed. Margo, perhaps seeing a moment of weakness or simply because it was Friday and she wanted the weekend to start, yelled out, "Motion to end the meeting!"

Everybody, except for Leg, raised their hands, and the meeting ended. Margo and Penelope were gone before anybody said another word and suddenly it was just me, God, and Leg alone in the room.

"Well, that was great," I said. "They seem really lovely."

"They're heinous," Leg said. "And I question their commitment to prom."

"Yeah, they're obviously only here for the clout," God said.

Leg looked at his friend and then turned back to me. "*Top Gun* prom aside, they treat Bri horribly, which you might think I would like because Bri also isn't very nice to me. But I see past all that. I'm a good person. And anyway, she just hasn't fully absorbed *Top Gun* prom. Yet."

"Yeah, give her time," I said, and God chuckled. "So, they're mean to Bri?"

"They're holy rollers," God said. "They're horrible to everybody."

I tried to imagine Margo, Penelope, and Bri hanging out together and couldn't. Plenty of people had relationships that fizzled out once you went crossed the threshold of Central's doors. Even so, they seemed like complete opposites. While they might be "holy rollers," they were the quintessential type of girls that I had tried to avoid, nice but with an edge that always bordered on mean.

"Hey, Julie—" Leg was waving his hand in my face. "Could you talk to Bri? Maybe just vouch for me? For *Top Gun* prom? Or at the very least for how much I care about prom?"

"My man does love prom," God said. "*Top Gun* or not."

He looked so sincere. When I nodded, he reached over and hugged me and told me I was literally the greatest human, ever.

"Besides maybe Jesus. Or Gandhi. I mean, you're probably on the list. That's what I'm saying."

This jabroni right here.

When I got home, Mom was sitting at the kitchen table, drinking a cup of tea and scrolling on her phone. A small suitcase was parked by the front door. I kicked it gently.

"What's this? Finally leaving me for a younger daughter?"

She didn't even look away from her phone. "I've almost got you out of the house. Doesn't make sense to trade you in now."

I sat next to her, and she pulled me into a side hug and kissed my forearm, which was weird and tickled. When I shivered, she went in again, and I couldn't pull away because she'd been working out five days a week and now had this freakish old lady strength.

"I love you. You know that, right?" Mom said.

"Yeah, of course," I said. "I love you, too."

"Are you going to be okay this weekend?"

Party.

"Yeah, Mom. Go and have fun at your romantic weekend."

Party! Don't tell your mother.

Mom huffed and rolled her eyes, showing me what she was looking at on her phone. The website was for an "Intentional Movement" retreat, an opportunity—I learned, by scrolling down—to rework the vitality in your body using the latest methods of—I was just spitballing— beloved intention and, of course, crystals. There was a hundred percent chance of throat chanting, men in linen pants, and women who spend most of their lives on yoga mats.

"Sounds . . . fun?"

"We'll be lucky if we have five minutes alone together," Mom said, taking her phone and putting it face down on the table. She closed her eyes and moved her lips silently, probably reciting one of her mantras. When she finished, she looks calmer. Resolute.

"Listen to me. I sound like a child."

"I mean, I assume you're sharing a room," I said.

It came out before I even realized I said it. Mom went rigid, a kid caught. And listen, though it wasn't like I really wanted to fully understand or accept the ramifications of such a statement, I was also tired of dancing around it.

"I don't know. Maybe. But maybe not. How do you feel about that, Julie?"

"I prefer to have entirely zero thoughts on this, Mom."

This guy too!

"I just . . . I like Scott. And I think he's going to be around for a while, you know? But it's important that you're okay. Well, the most important thing."

She opened her mouth to say more, but I bent over and pulled her up into a hug, as big an embrace as I could manage. As I held her, I felt how small she'd gotten—strong, yes. But still smaller and for some reason that worried me, as if she was going to eventually disappear, too. Whisked away by the wind.

"I'm good," I tell her. "I promise. Have fun with Scott. Don't do anything I would do."

A good one, Juliana. Top-notch.

Mom wiped away a tear. "Jesus, Julie. I just did my makeup."

When she had composed herself, she moved the hair out of my eyes and smoothed a few wrinkles on my shoulders. It was as if those were the only problems she could find, little fires put out easily enough. And I knew she wanted to tell me I sounded just like Dad, that I was just as bad, recycling his old jokes like cardboard memories. Sometimes it was intentional, but most of the time it wasn't. Instead, it was as if he'd somehow become a part of me, something deeper than simple DNA that came out when I needed it the most.

But Mom didn't say anything about Dad, maybe because she didn't want to ruin any more eye makeup or maybe because after years of saying it—of remembering him—she was finally ready to take the next step forward.

CHAPTER NINE

Scott picked Mom up about an hour later and they were both in such a hurry, I didn't get the usual Scott treatment, all the sunbeams, which was fine but also a bit disorienting because he was always so intentional about making sure I was cool with his presence. But he redeemed himself when he was pulling out of the driveway and yelled, "Namaste!" out the window.

There he is.

Even Mom seemed embarrassed by that.

Suddenly I was nervous about being alone. Part of me wanted to go running down the street, chasing Scott's Prius until Mom caught a glimpse of me in the rearview mirror, her only child—not ready to be alone after all. This feeling lasted until I turned around to go back into the house. Then something bigger than me took hold, old magic passed down from teenager to teenager since the beginning of time.

Possibility. A taste of freedom. And like so many teenagers before me, I embraced it—hard. Meaning, I flopped down on the couch and turned on the television for mindless scrolling through streaming services.

Old magic, indeed.

My phone lit up with a text from Max, which was only strange because it was peak Orange Julius hours.

Perhaps he needs us to visit him. Gas up the truck!

You heard from Bri?

It was exhausting to have people constantly checking in. In the thick of it, I told Mom I needed a neon sign to hang around my neck, blinking a message for everyone—"I assure you I am okay, just milking this dead dad thing for a day off school."

She didn't laugh, which was fine.

We use the tools we have available to us, Juliana.

I texted Max back: Think she just needed a day off

I fought the urge to add something like, "probably trying to get a break from your stalker ass" but poor Max was simply too pure for this world, so I dropped my phone onto the couch and tried to get back to truly embracing my freedom, committing to finding something mindless to watch and perhaps—*why not?*—thinking about ordering myself Door Dash. And yeah, at first it felt callous, but I was trying to convince myself—she just needed a day. Hell, I needed one yesterday. I even tried to do a version of Wentz's voice, with respect to Bri's solid impersonation—cracking myself up so much that it made me feel kind of lonely. The house a little emptier. Soon enough I flipped the channel and discovered a rerun of Adrenaline, getting lost in the beats of a storyline I knew by heart.

Somewhere between a haircut match and a surprise appearance by the Mad Capper—

An all-time worst gimmick

—I almost forgot that I'd been worried. That was, until Max showed up for his regular Friday night appointment—Adrenaline, live. He was early and about to break my door down with the way he was hammering on the thing.

"Max, unless Orange Julius has burned down, all of this is likely an overreaction."

Juliana! Bite your tongue!

Max gave me a quizzical look, as if somehow the loss of his part-time job at the Mall of America wouldn't be my number one concern. He shook it off and stepped inside.

"I think we should go over to Bri's house."

"Max, she's fine," I said. "And I think us showing up—or at least you showing up—might not be the message you want to put out into the world. Rings kind of stalker-ish."

This made Max think for a moment. "I'll risk it. It's like she fell off a cliff, Julie. So many texts that I had to mute her—don't tell her that, please—because the constant buzzing was keeping me up. And then all of a sudden, nothing. I texted her, like, ten times, and still nothing."

"You texted her ten times?" I asked.

Whatever was worrying Max trumped the embarrassment of being so obviously thirsty on main. And once again, I let it pass.

You're a near saint.

I'd never seen him this way before—strangely confident,

but also exposed in a vulnerable way that made me only love him more.

"I don't know where she lives," I said.

"Oh, I do. I looked it up."

"You looked it up."

"Yeah, of course."

Of course!

"Why?"

"I don't know. I wanted to know where she lived!"

Max saw me working through the shock of this revelation, slowly realizing that maybe he had done another thing wrong. He was concerned, the only emotion that could overtake the excitement that pulsed from his body ever since he'd met Bri. And I could tell that he was waiting for me to smother all this concern, the excitement, and for a moment it made me wonder if somehow, I'd always treated Max like dirt and only now realized it.

No, Juliana. You and Max are good.

"We're going to miss Adrenaline," I said. And immediately I wanted to take it back. It had come out all wrong. "I mean, we should. We can watch it later. I'm sorry."

"It's okay. I'm just . . . worried. You know?"

He looked sheepish, as if he'd surprised himself with the words. Before he could open his mouth again, I said, "I'll get my shoes."

Bri lived on Summit Avenue, a stretch of houses that are veritable mansions, the sort of old money literally found in

Gatsby novels. My dad used to say he couldn't afford to even drive down the avenue.

Big money.

Her house was large enough that I wasn't exactly sure which door we should knock on. However, Max took the lead and decided on a side door where a light was faintly showing from a stairwell in the distance. He knocked, rang the bell, and then knocked again—this time a little louder. The person who came down the stairs wasn't Bri but could be in about twenty years. She was probably the same age as Mom, put together and damn near glamorous even though she was wearing a velour track suit and looked to have just finished a workout. She was wiping her forehead and smiled when she saw us.

"Hi—" Max started. "We're, uh, friends? Of Bri's?"

Max shot me a look, obviously flustered. I took over. "Is Bri here? We were supposed to hang out, and we can't get in touch with her."

If her mom was surprised by us dropping by, she didn't show it. She pointed to the stairs behind her and said, "Just keep going until you get to the top!"

I followed Max up the steps, which spun around and around—four floors in total—until they spilled out into what used to be an attic but had been transformed into a huge room of slanted ceilings and little pocket areas with individual windows. In the middle, a sectional couch faced a wall with a giant flat-screen television.

"Hey!" Bri said, standing up. "What are you guys doing here?"

Suddenly I felt foolish. We barely knew this girl and there we were riding to her rescue in Max's Ford Focus like a couple of overzealous kids who'd seen one too many movies. I looked over to Max, who seemed to be navigating the same exact feelings.

"We, uh, were just—" Max looked to me for help. I tagged in yet again for my guy.

"We were worried about you," I said quickly, cringing. "Which, now, feels . . . kind of dumb."

Bri was taken aback. But then she looked like she was about to cry, but also kind of laughing as she wiped her eyes. She put down the bag of popcorn she was holding and sprinted toward us, gathering us together in a group hug.

"This is the nicest thing anybody has ever done for me," she said, which felt a bit overstated but whatever. "I'm fine. I just needed a day. But, ah!"

She hugged us again. And then, just like that, she was pulling us over to the couch and pressing Play on the remote. The television came alive with a movie I knew instantly.

"Talk to me, Goose!"

"*Top Gun*? The original?" Max asked, looking to me, as if maybe she had a secret eighties' movie obsession hidden right below the surface. "Not that I don't appreciate *Top Gun*—who doesn't?"

Bri sighed and shook her head.

"Anyway. Let's just turn it off. I don't want to think about *Top Gun* for one more second."

"What? Are you kidding," I said. "We came over to

check on you, but this is just a bonus."

"Uh, yeah. We are totally finishing this," Max said. He sat down next to her on the couch, put his arm around her, so damn casual.

This jabroni right here!

I stood there trying to process what I was seeing—*Top Gun* on the television, suave Max. The whole thing was surreal.

"Hey, Julie," Max said.

"What?"

"Are you going to stand there . . . or . . . ?"

Max cocked his head to the side, telling me to stop acting like a complete freak, not to ruin this for him, and to just sit the hell down.

I dropped down on the couch next to them. "My dad hated this movie. 'Nothing but American industrial war complex propaganda.'"

"The 'American industrial war complex.'" Max laughed. "Your dad was awesome."

In Dad's mind, it was canon. Fact. He'd shake his head when I'd see it on television and linger on the channel, loving it despite him. Sometimes to spite him.

"It's also the most unintentionally gay movie ever committed to film," Bri said.

Max grabbed the remote and pressed Pause. He took a second to gather himself.

"We are talking about the airplane movie, right?" Max asked.

"Jets," I clarified, but the point was valid.

Bri had transferred from Holy Angels, so who knows what they taught about pop culture icons over there.

Top God.

I laughed, and both Bri and Max were looking at me like I was a nut.

"But . . . you've seen this movie before?" I asked.

Bri grabbed the remote from my hand and hit Fast Forward, speeding through the scenes until Maverick and Goose and all their oiled, well-muscled and shirtless friends were standing—inexplicably—on the beach, playing volleyball.

"Watch this scene. How can anybody watch this movie and conclude that Maverick and his friends are straight?"

Bri pressed Play and let the scene play out—a scene that had always been innocuous to my innocent eyes—was suddenly a sultry, over-the-top metaphor for all things sexual. By the time the actual sex scene occurred, it felt almost pedestrian.

"I will never watch this movie the same way again," Max said.

"What can I say," Bri said. "Catholic school changes you."

The night turned into a marathon before we knew it, and halfway through the next movie, Max was snoring lightly on Bri's shoulder. I didn't know why I felt protective of him, but she seemed to embrace the totality of Max.

He slept through the credits and I half expected Bri's

mom to come upstairs and tell us it was time to leave. Instead, Bri put on another movie, carefully sitting down on the couch just as the opening fanfare opening played. It was a bank heist movie of some kind. I had never seen it.

"I appreciate you coming over," she said. "Thank you."

"Well, it was all Max," I said, which didn't feel like the truth but also wasn't a lie. Max had been swept away, completely off his feet. It made me smile. Bri, too.

"I love how close you two are," she said.

"Maybe too close sometimes."

She laughed and Max stirred. Both of us watched him and once he was settled, Bri started talking again.

"I used to have this whole group of friends," she said. "Youth group friends."

She swallowed and forced a smile.

"You met two of them—when we were hanging up the sign."

On first glance, Margo and Penelope weren't much different from Bri. And had I never spoke to Bri again, I wouldn't have been able to differentiate them if I'd seen them in the hallway. But even my limited interaction with Margo and Penelope in the prom meeting today told me they were not the same.

"Ah, yeah. They were at the prom meeting."

Bri didn't say anything, just stared at the television before seeming to rally herself. But her normal enthusiasm was tapped.

"You went to the meeting?"

"Yes," I said.

"Were the idiots there?"

"Leg and God? Yes. They tried to get a vote of no confidence in enchanted gardens."

"And did they mention . . ."

"*Top Gun* prom? Yes."

"That is literally the worst idea ever," Bri said, her voice raising momentarily. Both of us looked at Max, who was dead to the world. "*Top Gun* prom can't be my legacy, Julie."

"Margo moved to adjourn the meeting, so we didn't vote on anything."

Something new flickered on Bri's face. She shook her head and said, "Yeah, so Margo and Penelope were already at Central when I got here. And I thought, great—youth group friends! Some things happened at Holy Angels, and I thought coming to Central would help, but . . ." She waved her hands in the air dismissively, like she was trying to ward off tears. "My mistake, I guess."

She fiddled with a piece of loose fabric on one of the quilts. "Our whole youth group used to hang out at Memory Lanes a lot. That was our turf."

"Your turf?" I couldn't stop my voice from breaking with laughter. "I'm sorry, I really am. But it's just so . . ."

"Christian school. I know." Bri laughed; this time it even sounded genuine. "It was like the one place where our parents would let us hang out, alone, because it's owned by a church member."

Bri turned back to the movie, reaching down and picking up a piece of popcorn. She ate it, then a few more before putting the bag aside and pulling her legs up to her chest.

"So, what happened?" I asked. Subtlety and general politeness had never been in my top five traits and, let's face it, I wanted to know. "I mean, you don't have to tell me. I'm sorry."

Bri shook her head without missing a beat. "I had sex."

"Uh . . . that's it? Wait. Was it the kid who was going to be the youth pastor?"

"No, not him. That had already . . . ended. Just some guy. Which is even worse, I guess."

"But . . . that's it. You had sex."

"The fact that you're not scandalized by this makes me all the happier that we are"—she looked away—"friends."

I had many, many questions. If anything, my parents had been too sex positive—Mom would hate me even saying that, but it had been weird at times. Like, too frank. Too transparent. But it worked because the idea of being scandalized by anything sexual was, honestly, a mystery.

"I mean, yeah. Cool. I just—sorry, I just don't get the crisis."

"You have to grow up in that world to understand, I guess. Not that I'm trying to excuse all of that purity shit. But you live in that world and it's built inside you, brick by brick—*Don't have sex! Jesus is watching!*"

"Weird. And maybe kind of gross?"

Bri chuckled humorlessly. "Either way, I transferred to

Central and the gossip followed. There's Bri, the girl who ruined her life."

She didn't say anything else for a few minutes. The house creaked with the wind, which had begun to pick up outside. Downstairs her mother had turned off the lights, making it seem like we were even more alone than we were.

"Anyway, I thought helping plan the prom would be a distraction, I guess? Or maybe it would help Margo and Penelope see I'm still me? But the whole thing is just becoming more and more pointless. Especially now that I've got to deal with an infestation of skaters."

"For what it's worth, I think they come in peace."

"They want a *Top Gun* prom, Julie," she said. It was the way she said it, exasperated but like she'd just told me ghosts were real. We both cackled and it woke up Max, whose sheer confusion about being in a dimly lit attic instead of his own bed was exacerbated by me and Bri laughing even louder.

"I can't help that I have sleep blindness!" Max said, pushing me into the cushions of the couch. "I wonder what it's like to have friends that are actually nice to you?"

Sleep blindness? More like candy-ass-ivitus!

Bri leaned close to Max and kissed him, lightly and on the lips. Was it their first kiss? Max looked as if the entire universe had suddenly unfolded in front of him. I wanted to believe that he would look that way every time they kissed, hokey or not. I was still staring at them, I guess, because he turned to me and asked, "Why are you leering at me?"

"What? I'm not. Leave me alone."

"I fall asleep for a few minutes and suddenly the whole vibe gets weird."

"Hours," Bri clarified, and a sudden flash of horror crossed Max's face. Bri leaned over and kissed him again. That same look of wonder. That same joy. He kissed her back and I had to clear my throat because I wasn't going to just sit here while they made out.

"Okay, you need to leave," Bri said. And at first I thought she was talking to me, but she pushed Max off the couch as she said, "You're too cute and you're making Julie uncomfortable."

"A little harsh, but show me the lie," Max said, standing and stretching. He gathered his jacket and phone and then, incredibly, with no context or warning, he gave us a full-on, curtain call bow.

"What was that?" I asked him.

"Nothing. Don't worry about it. I'm tired and it's messing with my ability to read social situations. I'm leaving now. Last chance if you want a ride."

My knee-jerk responsibility almost made me grab my jacket and follow Max to the car. But just as quickly one question—one word—popped into my head. Why? Mom wasn't home. It was Friday night. This wasn't unsafe. I didn't need to care for any pets. And I wanted to be here.

"I'm good," I said.

"Okay, cool," Max said, walking to the stairs. "But for the record, not letting me stay for a sleepover might be sexist. Reverse sexism! I'll discern and get back to you."

This is not a thing, Max.

"Please tell us what you come up with," I said.

"We'll definitely wait up," Bri said.

But she still ran over to Max and pulled him into one final kiss, followed by another one and then a third before she literally tore herself away from him and came giggling back to the couch.

"Okay. Well. Just so you know, that will definitely not influence, uh, my research."

He nodded and then looked at his feet for a second or two, perhaps waiting for us to fold—to tell him to stay. When no invitation came, he muttered something to himself and then gave us a salute.

"Jesus, I don't know why I just did that. Goodbye."

And then he was gone.

CHAPTER TEN

I woke up to the smell of something sweet and warm—cinnamon rolls. When I made my way down to the kitchen, Bri and her mother were standing hip to hip at the stove, giggling about something. They looked close, happy. A snapshot from *Midwest Living* or some other magazine you'd see in the grocery store.

I cleared my throat and they both turned around and let's just say that Bri came by her personality naturally. Her mom was all over me, trying to tend to every possible need. It would've been annoying if it wasn't so sweet.

"I'm going to tell your dad breakfast is ready," her mom said. "Feel free to make some coffee if you want it."

Bri turned and gave me a tired smile. Before she could say anything, the doorbell rang and I followed her to the front door, where Max was standing sheepishly with three coffees.

"Aw," Bri said, and Max blushed. "Look at you. You're already so whipped."

"Yeah," I said. "Look at you."

When Bri leaned into kiss Max, I raised my eyebrows as if to say, *I see you, Max. I* see you.

Max, you high-steppin' forward-thinkin' man of the people!

Max cleared his throat. "Well, anyway. I just figured you all stayed up late talking about me and so you might need some caffeine."

Bri's mom came up behind us said, "Aw! Look at you!"

This really got Max's color up, to the point that even he must have been able to feel it, because he coughed and stared at the floor.

"I figured we could take the coffee and maybe go out to Raspberry Island or something. Julie and I went there a lot as kids."

"I love that place," Bri said, looking at me.

"That sounds awesome," I said. "Cold, maybe. But awesome."

Bri smiled and grabbed her hat.

"Well, you kids have fun, but first . . . ," her mom said, holding up a finger before she jogged to the kitchen. A few moments later she had three small, covered plates—one for each of us—with a still-hot cinnamon roll inside. She gave Bri a kiss and then, surprising both me and Max, went in for hugs. If this embarrassed Bri, she didn't let it show. All she said was, "Thanks, Mom."

When we got to the car, Max let the engine run while he lifted the foil off his plate and smelled the cinnamon roll the way a person might appreciate a glass of fine wine. Eyes closed, everything. Bri and I shared a moment, both of us highly amused, until he finally opened his eyes and took a bite.

When he noticed us watching him, he said, "Oh God, what now?"

"I don't think I've enjoyed anything like you enjoyed the smell of that cinnamon roll," I said.

He shook his head, set the plate on the dashboard, and put the car into gear. He was still shaking his head as he backed out of Bri's driveway and into the road.

"Get somebody who looks at you the way Max looks at pastries," Bri said.

"I'm so glad I came over. . . ." Max sighed, but it didn't stop me or Bri. Max gunned his engine and sped down the road, but no amount of velocity could stop this.

"Seriously, dough," Bri said.

"The ladies need to know about . . . how you roll."

"Oh! Donut cry over this, it's all friendly," Bri said.

"God. You are so dumb," Max said as he made the final turn toward the river and Raspberry Island. "But don't expect me to laugh! Even if I respect your pun game."

The synonym for cinnamon roll is candy-ass!

Bri reached forward from the back seat and touched Max's shoulder.

"We're just messing with you," she said, grinning. "Don't be mad."

"I don't get mad," Max said. "I get even."

"Oh, Baby Jesus," I said.

"What?"

"I get even." Look at this tough guy.

"When have you ever gotten even in your entire life?" I asked.

Max finally broke. He took a big bite from the cinnamon roll, and through a mouthful of frosting and pastry said, "It's more of an unrequited getting even."

This made Bri erupt into laughter that would make you think Max was the funniest person she'd ever encountered, which I guaranteed wasn't the case. I was rolling my eyes so hard I swore the seat tilted back. When we parked across the street from the small strip of Raspberry Island, Bri leaned forward and planted a huge kiss on his cheek. Max didn't say anything, just smiled—big, like a single star on a dark night—and we opened our doors and went outside.

It was colder down by the water. We walked along the postage-stamp–sized park, nothing more than a brush of grass with a bandshell and a couple of park benches dotting the sides. Still, during the summer, these two acres were usually packed with picnickers, people looking to escape the noise of the city, and wedding after wedding.

"Why do we live on Hoth?" I asked.

"It's not that cold," Max said casually, as if I hadn't also grown up in Minnesota. As if he wasn't visibly shivering right in front of us. Still, we were weeks away from prom—and then graduation. And yet, if it snowed right now I wouldn't be surprised. It was cold. I was cold.

"I'm freezing," Bri confirmed. "But this is fun. I love it

here. It's a random island in the middle of the city."

Raspberry Island had no raspberries and Dad told me that when he was a kid, it was kind of a barren place—even used as a parking lot for a while. But then the city dumped some money into it, a reclamation project. Proof that even the most desolate and overgrown place could find new life.

"My dad used to bring me down here to see how fast we could run across the island without falling into the water," I said.

"Once again, your dad balancing awesomeness and risk management," Max said.

Bri hesitated. "So how long has he been, uh, gone?"

"Three years," I said.

Max looked at me, his eyes asking if he needed me to change the subject.

"Sometimes it feels a lot longer. I guess sometimes it feels like we've created this whole new life where he's more of a memory than something real. I don't know how to explain it."

"I'm . . . that's really sad," Bri said, sounding a little choked up.

"Oh God, I'm sorry," I said, suddenly embarrassed. "I have a tendency to, like, take it to eleven."

"No, no—it's not that. It's just. Most people are always, 'My parents are so stupid—blah, blah, blah.' And, I don't know, what you said was just different."

"Her dad was awesome," Max said, reaching over and touching my shoulder gently. It might've been weird. I might've given him the business for it any other time. But not right then. "He was just . . . awesome. That's all you can say about him."

"I mean, not always." I laughed. "He had no fear. Or sense of impropriety. So, he would, like, suddenly start telling cashiers at the grocery store about how Mom was actually a veteran of some early nineties' women's professional wrestling company— S.L.A.M. And Mom would deny it, of course, which made it seem even more plausible."

"Uh . . . what's S.L.A.M.?" Bri asked

"Sexy Ladies at Midnight," Max said. "It's on YouTube. We can watch it sometime."

The ass-kickin' Athenas from parts unknown. Woo!

"And he'd like . . . do the voices? Right there in the cashier line? I was thirteen."

Bri laughed. "So, 'awesome' is being used graciously here."

"I loved it," Max said. And then, all of a sudden, something about Max changed. He shot up from the bench like he'd been stung by something. I, too, jumped up and checked for—what? I didn't even know what to expect on such a cold morning on Raspberry Island.

"What the hell is wrong with you?" I asked.

"Oh God! You didn't see Adrenaline last night!"

"No . . ." And as much as I loved wrestling, I kind of wanted to yell at Max and be like, *Bro, I am a girl. I was at a sleepover.* Instead, I played it casual and said, "I'll catch up later."

"I got up early and watched it this morning."

He grinned—like he knew a secret. I was immediately caught between wanting to know and to run off screaming to avoid any spoilers. Or tackle him to the ground for being such a fanboy about this in front of Bri.

Before, Dad would get the same look. He never looked them up; he was a different kind of addict. But he seemed to just know how matches would end up, still enjoying the peaks and valleys of each match. Laughing at the way I lived and died with every heel turn. Every single angle. Because even though he knew the websites, the podcasts, he could never bring himself to cheat—and that was how he raised me to think about it, too. Cheating. Yourself, mostly, by breaking kayfabe—losing the chance to truly be surprised, a rarity that was almost invaluable now. Max gave me the business for it, even today. He was top fan on pretty much every message board, every subreddit. He always knew what was happening before the announcers did, but he understood why I wanted to keep it somewhat holy.

Rule number one: never break kayfabe, Juliana.

And maybe now more than ever, I didn't want to, at least in that one small way. I wanted to be able to say that this—this one part of my life—could still be ridiculous, a mystery, filled with sometimes incomprehensible storylines and characters that you never saw coming. I wanted to share this one last thing with Dad.

"Okay, well, we need to get off this island and get you to a TV stat."

"Stat, okay," I said.

This jabroni needs an atomic drop! Stat!

The realization that we weren't alone dawned on both Max and me at the same time. We both looked at Bri, who was still sitting on the bench watching all . . . this unfold. Normally we knew enough to clam up when an outsider was around. It wasn't that professional wrestling was embarrassing—

Juliana. Don't you say it.

I'm sorry, but it wasn't the sort of thing people continued to care about once they hit high school. At least, that was my and Max's experience. So, we avoided getting all breathless—in public—talking about how the Butcher showed up on Adrenaline when he was still signed to some promotion out of, like, Dubai.

Hard lessons.

And honestly? It was kind of fun having a secret passion—something that only Max and I understood. I knew he was going to show up at my house at nine p.m. on the dot every Friday night. And he knew that if he was even a minute late, he might as well turn around and go home.

We went hard. We were real heads, true believers.

That is exactly how I would describe you and Max.

But we had missed last night and neither of us had thought about it once. I wasn't sure how to process that information.

Bri stood up, an unreadable look on her face, and then essentially attacked Max. It wasn't a wrestling move exactly. It was more aggressive than that, honestly. It looked like what somebody thinks a wrestling move should look like, but only if they've never actually seen a wrestling match in their life. And slowly, but not slowly enough for anybody—ahem, like me—who might be sitting here watching, it turned into kind of a make-out session. I coughed a few times and Bri got the message. So her attack on Max ended with her sitting so close to him on the bench that she might as well have been on his lap. Max's hair was mussed, the collar of his T-shirt twisted sideways on his neck. He looked like he'd been fighting the Banshee, a lesser-known heel who never got over, essentially because her finishing move was to scream as loud as she could in her opponent's face.

I shake my head.

I laughed. And when they both looked at me, I just thought about the Banshee more.

"What's your problem?" Max said, a sliver of smile beginning to appear at the corners of his mouth. Maybe because we had some sort of best-friend ESP, he could see the ridiculous image of the Banshee imprinted on my brain. Or maybe because he knew this new normal, being attacked by somebody who wouldn't even know his name if this were a teen movie, was ridiculous. Or maybe that was how this movie played out—the nice guy, the pretty girl.

What a reversal!

And then something shifted, a new filter for what I was seeing. It was subtle; you could miss it completely if you weren't paying attention. But I liked to consider myself the foremost Max scholar and the way he was smiling was more than just having some hot girl attack him at a local park by the river.

"You guys are totally going to go to prom together," I blurted out. Max's entire body went rigid. Bri wasn't much better. They both looked to the ground, as if an answer was lost in the grass.

"Oh. Damn. I was thinking about teen movies and the Banshee—you remember her, Max?—and that just kind of came out. Damn. Did I say that yet? I'm sorry."

Get some, Max!

Max coughed. "Well, I mean, it's only logical."

Logical? Logical. That was his move. Well, that murdered any embarrassment I might've had. Now it was just watching Max stumble through a prom invite. I swear, somewhere above the din of the city, I could just make out the vaguely British narrator of a children's wildlife show, "And here, we get to see the rare mating ritual of . . . Max."

A-giantina Chokis Jobber.

"Well, I mean . . . you can't argue with . . . logic . . ." Bri couldn't look up and neither could Max. It was the worst staring contest of all time because each of them kept sneaking looks at the other, horrified when either would make eye contact. But it was also, perhaps, the sweetest thing I'd ever seen in my entire life.

Just ask her, you candy-ass!

"Just kiss again already."

I wish I'd suggested something else because they really

went for it. Enough that, from somewhere across the street an errant "Woo!" floated toward us.

Woo! Indeed!

"Okay, I'm gonna just . . ." I motioned across the park, but they were barely even aware that I was alive, let alone standing up to leave. I paused, but it was a big old goose egg for Julie. Nothing, not a word. "Okay . . . bye?"

I take it all back. Max, you've done me proud, brother!

I walked across the park, toward a group of people who were congregating near the band shell. It felt colder as the wind picked up, and I tried to wrap my arms around myself more. Tried to conjure the warmest memory possible—one from this actual place. Picnics or playing Pokémon Go. I didn't realize I'd gotten close to the crowd of people until I was basically standing next to Dr. Palmer, my sophomore year language arts teacher, who was eyeing me curiously.

"Julie? Are you here for the medieval armor demonstration?"

"Um, no?"

Dr. Palmer and her husband were setting up for a video shoot and had seemingly drawn a crowd. She handed me what could only be described as a tunic, which wouldn't win me any fashion contests but was a heavy wool and warm.

"Thank you," I said. "How's the, uh, YouTube game?" I asked.

"Oh, you know, it's all about the algorithms. We're actually doing more over on TikTok these days."

I didn't know what to say about that, which also didn't

really matter because Palmer was continuing on about how their particular audience—medieval enthusiasts—didn't have the short attention spans of normal social media consumers.

Palmer laughed as she said this, a joke.

"But TikTok creates the content for you. We just follow the trends, you know."

"I'm mostly on professional wrestling TikTok these days."

I intended for this to be a joke because I was not, in fact, on pro wrestling TikTok—or even sure it existed—but Palmer definitely didn't get it. She shook her head, as if to clear the distraction.

"So, what are you doing out here so early?"

Filming a wrestling TikTok, you jabroni—what do you think?

"I'm with Max and Bri." They were still all over each other. For a moment I saw Dr. Palmer's teacher brain activate. Vague disapproval passed over her face before she turned to me again and smiled.

"Well, they seem . . . occupied. Want to give us a hand on our shoot? We can always use some smart helpers."

Palmer was one of those teachers who had a preternatural ability to get you plugged into something before you knew what you were doing. She and Wentz were cut from the same cloth. Good people, but annoying in their design. Dr. Palmer was there for me after my dad died, suffering through lunches where she let me come to her room and read possibly some of the worst poetry that had ever been written, grief or not. She listened attentively, chewing on each saccharine word—and some of them were page-turning epics—before pulling her reading glasses off her nose and saying, "You are definitely exploring a theme."

What a response! You'd be right if you noticed there was nothing in there about them being good. Instead, she simply acknowledged that, in fact, words with a discernible theme had been put on paper. A newborn could probably write a poem with a theme. But that was the beauty and grace of Dr. Palmer. She took you seriously, even when you were begging not to be.

"I think I'm just going to walk around until they tire themselves out," I said.

Palmer glanced across the park and then back at me. "It looks like it might be a minute."

No lies detected, Juliana!

She reached over, adjusted the tunic around my shoulders, and said, "Keep this and just get it back to me next week—okay?"

"Okay, thanks."

I was about to walk away when Palmer went in for a hug, which was a breach of school etiquette—maybe even a law—because she stopped herself just short of an actual hug and said, "It's just really good to see you out, Julie. With people. Dare I say having fun, even. Spoiler alert: this is what life is really about."

I nodded because I didn't know what to say. Yes, I felt better. And yes, I was able to walk around, to play the role of the normal high school kid most of the time. But I wondered if people like Mom, teachers like Dr. Palmer and Wentz, and even Max, ever secretly wondered if their lives were just a big angle, some kind of elaborate heel turn that would eventually get exposed when the audience least expected it.

In the earliest days of wrestling, people believed it was real because, for the most part, it was—grudge matches that lasted hours, true tests of endurance that could be won or lost on the smallest technical moves. Slowly, through the years, promoters wised up and started leaning more heavily on the entertainment than the sports side of the promotion. But it was years—decades, in certain parts of the world—before people wanted to be let in on the joke. Before they wanted to know that it was fake.

The lie was better than reality.

Dad always said we wanted to believe in things bigger than ourselves. We needed to believe that things weren't just being scripted by a guy standing just behind the curtain backstage.

"Oh shit! Julie? Are you a part of the storm mob?!"

Leg and God had appeared. A few people in the crowd shouted a "What—WHAT!" at them, to which they both responded with a fist pump.

"What the hell is a storm mob?" I asked.

Leg looked disappointed, God amused. "Dr. Palmer's official set of groupies," God said. "For her weird videos."

"What—WHAT!" Leg yelled, which got an immediate response from the group.

"And so . . . you guys always show up?"

"It's kind of become a thing," God says.

"We're, like, the leaders, if you go by a certain rubric," Leg said. "Unofficially, of course."

Max walked up and said, "Oh, so kind of like the prom committee?"

It wasn't the best first impression, and I didn't know how to interpret what I was feeling inside either—like my stomach had dropped, just an inch or so. But enough that I gave Max a look.

"We filled out the paperwork," Leg said, looking past Max to Bri, who was trying her best not to get pulled into this conversation. "Oh, I see—the prom dictator is your girlfriend? I see you, Bri! Liberate prom!"

"'Liberate prom'?" God laughed.

"Whatever, it's borderline fascism having to fill out a form to be in a school club," Leg said. "You can't ignore the people!"

Bri shook her head and pulled out her phone. God laughed again and started rubbing his friend's shoulders like a boxer getting ready for the next round.

"For what it's worth, I never filled out the paperwork . . . ," I said.

Leg looked dumbfounded.

God put an arm around his friend. "Thank you for ensuring that would be the only thing I'll hear about the rest of the weekend."

Then Max piped in again. "Well, this is awkward.

Because I guess I am on the prom committee? As of, like, two minutes ago?"

"I know this guy didn't fill out the paperwork," Leg said, obviously disappointed by the broken system. "But listen, I know she's, like, your girlfriend. Just think about it: *Top Gun* prom."

About that time the storm mob started cheering and Leg—legitimately conflicted—looked from them, back to us, and then back to the mob, which was cheering on what looked to be a demonstration of hand-to-hand fighting techniques.

"Anyway, be on the right side of history, man. Do it for the people."

"The people," God agreed.

And with that, they ran off to join the mob. A loud "What—WHAT" greeted them just as they joined the ranks.

Max cleared his throat.

"That was weird," he said.

"I like them."

He gave me a strange look, one I'm not sure I'd seen from him before. Like he was about to ask a series of probing questions. "What? They're nice. And funny."

"Mm-hmm." Max studied my face a few more seconds and then said, "Well, good news and bad news."

"Okay . . ."

"Good news—we're going to prom." He said it almost sheepishly. "And I wasn't lying to your guy. Because, bad news, I am, in fact, now on the prom committee. And I guess now I know why."

Your guy Leg?

I cleared my throat.

"Yes. Yes, you do. And how did that happen?"

Max shook his head and laughed. "I guess the sort of devil's wager that I'd have to enter into to get somebody like Bri to take me to prom."

"Stop," I said. Max looked at me, waiting for the surprise left hook that almost always came next. But I wasn't swinging. Not now. "You deserve somebody exactly like Bri."

"Well . . . thank you. But it's also kind of improbable. Especially all the making out."

Here was the thing about me and Max. I could say anything to him. When we lost Dad, he was the first person at our house. When the last casseroles came out of the freezer and the well-wishers and prayer-sayers stopped talking to the sky, there was Max—nudging me to watch Adrenaline. Describing how he was trolling the subreddits with unhinged storylines that, when challenged, he'd say came from "solid sources," enraging the posters even more. But I didn't know how to tell Max any of this, or to tell him that he and Bri weren't an anomaly.

They were hope. They were what people talk about when they talk about faith and courage and all that happy business that, if it weren't for him, I wouldn't be able to believe in. I wanted to tell him that he deserved every single minute of happiness he was getting. He deserved a person like Bri, who seemed to be just as blessedly unhinged as he was.

Tell him all of that, Juliana. Right now.

But I couldn't get the words out, or maybe didn't know how. Instead, I looked down and he stepped a little closer to me, shivering.

"Well, I still think the making out is improbable," Max said, laughing. "And hey, uh, what's with the . . . tunic?"

"Long story. But if you're nice, I'll let you borrow it for prom."

"I'll probably just get the Orange Julius uniform washed and pressed. I think she's hot for it."

"Oh, those are words I never need to hear again."

Right then, Bri joined us, slipping her arm around Max's waist and nestling her head into the crook of his neck. We stood there watching the waves of the Mississippi River—just breaking away from the frozen winter ice—roll against the banks of the small island, the sounds of a medieval TikTok being filmed behind us.

CHAPTER ELEVEN

When I got home, the house was cold and empty. I got Adrenaline queued up on the television and sat on the couch, but something about the shadows, about suddenly being alone, was working on me. Max had gone to Orange Julius and Bri's mom—upon hearing the happy news about prom—wanted to take her shopping for a dress. They had asked me to go but as nice and genuine as they were, it was an invitation anyone knew to decline. The sort of thing a mom and a daughter should do together. So, I was alone and hungry, and I guess that's how I decided that the responsible thing to do would be to seek out actual human contact and have dinner at the Mall.

Let's gooooo!

The Mall wasn't busy and neither was Max, who had managed to separate himself from Bri's lips long enough to make it to his shift. I told him as much.

"Nice to know the goodwill from Raspberry Island has dissipated," he said, handing me the two cups.

I took a long-ass sip of the Orange Julius and said, "Ahhh!"

"Could you be more annoying?" he said.

"What would you do without me?" I asked. "I speak the truth into your life."

Somebody call nine-one-one! This guy needs a candy-ass-ectomy!

"What truth? Half the stuff you say is objectively not true. It's just stuff you literally make up!"

"You love me. I mean, not as much as Bri. Because kissy-kissy and all that. But you know you love me."

He grimaced. I took another long-ass sip.

"Ahhh."

Look at this lovestruck, wobbly-kneed, candy-assed so-and-so.

"Julie, sometimes I really do not like you. I need you to know this," Max said. "It's an aggressive dislike."

One more sip.

"Don't you do it—"

Ahhh!

I raised my eyebrows, finishing one more long pull on the bright orange straw. Maybe he was waiting for me to take back what I'd said on the island. I still didn't have the words, so I reached across the counter and squeezed his hand. It was weird, but I wasn't exactly sure what else to do, since I surely couldn't trust myself from turning it all around and delivering one more joke like a surprise suplex. Because, c'mon! This sudden turn to Mr. Lady Killer Extraordinaire or whatever? This was a storyline not even a true believer could find credible.

Not one bit, jabroni.

"I'm just messing with you," I finally said. "And besides, if I make you mad, I'd have to go back to my house. That's why I ended up here anyway. It's all sad and lonely at old *mi casa*."

A huge, wonder-filled smile came across his face.

"Anyway, stop burying the lede. Can you believe it?"

"Believe what?"

He dropped his hands to his sides. "Uh, Adrenaline? You watched it, right?"

"Not yet, but I will."

He held up his hands. If I tried opening my mouth, he shushed me, which was usually enough to be on the wrong end of the people's elbow, but he was out of range.

"I'm not talking to you until you watch Adrenaline," he said. "Go watch it on your phone. And then report back to me."

"Max, I'll watch it later. I just want to talk—"

He shushed me again and then a third time when I said that I had certain philosophical standards around watching professional wrestling on my phone in a food court in the Mall of America. But he was resolute, turned his back on me. Started cleaning the machines, which felt especially aggressive given the Mall wouldn't close for another two hours. I picked up the second Orange Julius with a sigh and walked toward the escalator.

From behind me I heard him yell, "Report back! To me!"

There were two food courts in the Mall of America, the one on the north side of the building, full of newfangled restaurants and hip reality television cake shops and such.

And then there was the real food court, the OG, on the south side of the Mall. Depending on where you sat you could see the amusement park, or you could find yourself inside what could only be described as a tunnel of restaurants connecting one side of the food court to the other. It was some modern-day Willy Wonka business, at least to me. At the end of the tunnel was a chain coffee shop that, if you were a Mall veteran, you knew had the perfect place to sit. A little nook of three to four small tables. Seemingly hidden from everybody else in the Mall, especially on a night like tonight.

I sat down and propped my phone against one of the Orange Julius cups. The girl behind the coffee shop counter gave me a look that I ignored because anybody who knew anything knew you didn't need to buy that weak coffee to sit in this spot. This was public domain, lady! Not controlled by you or your Moose Coffee overlords!

We are the Orange Julius mafia!

I popped in my earbuds and pressed play on the Adrenaline video. The intro music was a familiar friend—like seeing somebody from freshman year who'd been swallowed up and digested into nothingness by the AP and IB schedules. Over the years the intro music changed, but never significantly enough to lose the core ability to make true fans perk up anytime they heard it.

Right away I could tell the announcers—Axe Duggan, Steven "Sweet Time" Jones, and Bulldozer Jenkins—were in rare form. Yelling over the crowd, telling anyone who would listen that we were in for something special tonight, so special that you couldn't miss it. And couldn't you feel the energy? Weren't you ready to DDT some unsuspecting Moose Coffee employee through the table because you knew you were sitting in a public domain seating area, which was totally not owned by Moose Coffee?

Yeah, sure, I added that last bit, but let me tell you I was feeling it from the jump.

And that lady at the counter isn't saying nothing, Juliana. Tag me in! Woo!

The first match was over before it really started, a mini feud between two up-and-coming wrestlers that I still didn't have a solid opinion about. The storyline probably wouldn't ever develop. The second was a women's match that, despite the low-cut costumes and obvious pandering to the male gaze, was actually pretty good and, by the end of it, made me a fan of the loser of the match, Betty Boom—who, let me tell you, looked like she could seriously kick your ass, Moose Coffee Lady.

Yeaahhh, I'm looking at you, Espresso Girl!

Two more up, two more down—nothing special—so as the episode started to come to a close and Sweet Time Jones showed up in the ring with a microphone in hand, ready to do one of his meaningless end-of-show interviews, I couldn't help but think Max didn't know a good wrestling angle from a hole in the wall.

Sweet Time started like he always does, pumping up the crowd—always looking for a pop. He was one of those guys who looked like he actually got straight A's in school while also being, like, the starting quarterback. Plus, his entrance song sucked and had become a gigantic meme, which was unfortunate.

Damn those memes, Juliana.

And yet, when he said he had a special guest, I sat a little straighter. This was classic wrestling misdirection. Set the audience up with a seemingly innocuous situation—like, say, an interview. Let it go on for five, six minutes. Nothing to see here, right?

Wrong! Woo!

Suddenly somebody was running into the ring, or sneaking up behind the people doing the interview. Or maybe there was a heel turn coming—maybe even for Sweet Time himself, surprising us not only with the turn but also the return to the ring—posing as a double agent for, say, the Behemoth because they've secretly been looking to take the Adrenaline World Championship away from current champ and walking Ken doll Michael Stixx.

This is a good angle, Juliana.

Perhaps I was projecting, because when Stixx's entrance music started I almost shut off the video. I knew exactly what this was about. Another limping promo for Hell on the Hill, the next pay-per-view where Stixx would spend thirty minutes showing us how he was nothing but a pretty face, grooming himself like a long-haired, well-bred cat. It wasn't that I loathed his whole vibe—but it was definitely that, too—he was easily one of the worst technical wrestlers in the company. Just hair and a nice set of teeth. Not deserving of the heavyweight belt.

Jabronis all around us, Juliana.

Anyway, I barely listened to Stixx drone on about Hell on the Hill. Despite telling myself I wouldn't order it out of spite and principle, I knew Max would show up and we'd totally spend half his check on this damn thing.

Bunch of candy-ass, no-gimmick-havin'—

That was when it happened.

It's hard for non-wrestling fans to understand the way entrance songs are embedded into the DNA of a wrestling fan's mind and soul—something that could crack even the hardest dude in the audience and have him screaming like a kid at their first rock concert. And of course, Adrenaline knew this—they played this card every chance they could. Because everyone knew the golden rule of professional wrestling: a cheap pop was better than no pop at all.

The screen went pitch-black. Two strums of a distorted guitar. And that was all I needed. I jumped out of my chair, kicking it behind me—Espresso Girl gave me a look, but she couldn't possibly understand what was happening. When the house lights came back up on screen, there was The Legend—A Prototype of God's Own Making, Never Considered for Mass Production, smiling his smug-ass grin. Hair perfect, even though he'd been retired for how long? Microphone poised right in front of his mouth.

Legend? More like an out-to-pasture has-been!

But he couldn't say anything because the crowd was

losing their collective shit. Hell, I was losing it and the coffee girl was on the phone now, probably calling security, even though it was seven-thirty on a Saturday night, and any true Mall head knew they were already in the parking decks making sure people weren't taking advantage of the empty corners and lack of security cameras. Anyway, I couldn't even care right now, because The Legend was back. The Legend was back!

"Well, well, well."

The crowd, seriously. The crowd was giving me life, a collective of people who had been born again—baptized in the name of something wholly unexpected. The Legend kept bringing the mic to his lips, but the crowd could barely stand, couldn't do anything but scream. The Legend left at the peak of his popularity. Adrenaline's management had rigged a "loser leave town" match and one-two-three, The Legend was gone.

And, okay, listen. I knew he'd been in the middle of a contract dispute, wanting money akin to God. I knew he dropped "The Legend" after the second hit movie and now went simply by his name, Rob Heart, which is how I should've known him. But kayfabe, right? So, I didn't want to think about the greed or the way promotions chewed up and spit out talent, leaving most of them hobbled and working the convention circuits—a life of hustling twenty-dollar autographs.

The Legend held a hand up and this—this!—brought immediate silence. Nobody disrespected The Legend.

I disrespected his candy-ass multiple times, Juliana.

"It looks like this place is in serious need of a little . . ."

"HEART," everyone screamed, including maybe me—and I saw you, Coffee Lady, I saw you.

"Let's cut to the chase, Stixx. You. Me. Anytime. Anywhere."

The crowd was alive. A nightmare from under the bed, crawling up the walls. A living and breathing and screaming thing.

Stixx laughed because he was a smug prick—always had been—and because he knew how to work the crowd. He reached over, popped the lapel on Legend's suit, and then sniffed the air once, twice, before lifting the mic to his mouth.

"You smell like mothballs, old man. How old is that suit anyway?"

I gripped the backrest of my chair. I would hit Stixx, believe that. The Legend looked indifferent, though. He laughed and looked to the crowd as he motioned to Stixx, as if to say, *This jabroni!* Then, slowly, he pulled off his blazer. Followed by his vest, his shirt and tie, until he was standing in the ring, ready to brawl. He still looked like he'd been carved from granite, even at what had to be fifty years old.

"I'm free, you closet champion."

The crowd lost it and Stixx didn't like the accusation—even if he was a closet champion, unwilling to risk defending the belt. They were about to get it on when a host of referees and security guards flooded the ring, separating the two wrestlers. Sweet Time stepped between the two giants, microphone in one hand—a piece of paper in another. A contract.

"Gentlemen, let's settle this like men. Three weeks. Minneapolis. I have a contract right here. Are you in?"

I was caught by surprise. Three weeks? Minneapolis? A contract? None of this made sense.

Stixx grabbed the mic. "Maybe you can get yourself a new suit, old-timer. I hear there's a mall there."

Both men grabbed the contract, signed it, and slowly went nose to nose before the screen suddenly went black, save a title card announcing that professional wrestling was back at the Mall of America for the first time in nearly thirty years.

Tickets on sale now.

When Max saw me coming down the escalator, he raised his hands in the air and yelled, "THIS PLACE NEEDS A LITTLE . . ."

"Heart!" I called, although I couldn't bring myself to match his volume, even if the rotunda was essentially empty. When I got up to the counter, I couldn't contain my excitement.

"I told you!" he said.

"Shit. Did you know?"

Max shook his head, the excitement alive on his face. "I mean, there was some chatter that somebody was coming back. At first, I thought it might be the Breathtaking One. I think he still might end up on the card, though, because it's the same weekend of his book signing and . . . that's just too convenient. But, Julie, I'm not going to lie. When the walk-out music played? I cried."

I couldn't tell if he was being serious, but I didn't care. My entire body was humming. I felt like I could run through a brick wall.

"I almost had to drop-kick a mall worker," I said.

"What?"

"Nothing, don't worry about it."

"Anyway . . . nobody knew it was coming to the Mall," he said. "That was a total surprise."

Dad had told me the stories too many times to count—back when the Mall was still in its infancy—another gimmick for the wrestling storylines. All four floors of the rotunda were full, standing room only, a tower of fandom reaching high above the ring. When he spoke about it, it was with nothing short of reverence. As if he had been witness to history—and he had. It wasn't the sort of history many people cared about, sure. But it was history he could pass down to me, an inheritance in the form of a VHS tape. Knowing that, somewhere on that blurry screen, he was there—even now. And for that alone, it was special.

"We should go," I said, the excitement building inside me. "We have to go!"

Max sighed. His entire body deflated. "Sold out. Like, immediately. I tried this morning, Julie."

Something inside me dropped. Adrenaline had come to

town before and we'd never tried to get tickets. It was just better in our living room, in almost every way. Maybe it was thinking about how Dad had gone, wanting to make that same connection. A kind of bookend that might offer some relief. Or maybe it was the shock of The Legend, the flirtation of the Breathtaking One being on the card. I don't know but I wasn't surprised. Minnesota, in many ways, was the genesis—the creation narrative—of modern professional wrestling. The roots here were deep. And while it was disappointing, I bounced back quick enough. All I wanted to do was go home, put on the first Mall match—prepare with integrity.

"Plus . . . it's on prom night." Max spoke carefully. "So. You know."

"Ah, well. I understand. Listen, you can make it up to me by coming over tonight when you get off. We need to watch the Mall match. And of course, grudge matches one, two, and maybe three—but everybody knows that one doesn't hold up as well."

Max went even stiffer and started wiping down the counter, which you could already eat off in its current state. "Uh, I have, uh, plans. But I can cancel them."

Well, shit.

Young love, dear.

Shit, shit, shit.

I paused just long enough that it was impossible that he didn't realize I'd forgotten about Bri, or at the very least that I had not switched off the "always available" light on our friendship—one that had always been on, no matter what, for as long as I'd known him. So, I turned the ship, fast.

"What? Max, please. The last thing you need is to come over to watch pro wrestling when you and Bri can go do—" I stopped myself. I didn't want to continue, which made me start laughing. "Whatever it is you all are going to do. It's cool. No details necessary."

He watched me, perhaps looking for even the smallest hint of disappointment—or worse, grief. Outside of the Mall match, the grudge matches were Dad's all-time favorites. Even as an unabashed Masked Man fan, it was difficult not to put some respect on The Legend during those matches. He was undeniably at the top of his game. Still, nobody hated The Legend quite like Dad.

A spotlight-stealin', pressed-pants, backhand-dealin' son of a bitch.

The fact that the Masked Man had never come back always felt like a gift. Dad died having seen it all, which I know sounds hokey, but I held on to that fact tightly. Sometimes, though, it felt like he had missed too much. I'd catch myself wanting to fill him in on the latest storylines, only to remember that he wasn't at home. Was no longer a text away. I remember the first Friday night without him and it wasn't sadness, not specifically. More like emptiness. Loss. Everything moved on, no matter what.

I need an Orange Julius.

CHAPTER TWELVE

All the lights were on at the house, and it unnerved me at first. I had definitely left the house dark, sad, and lonely. I opened the door slowly, ready to run and scream, only to find Mom on the couch, scrolling on her phone.

"What are you doing here?" I asked.

She put her phone down and sighed, calling me to her. She ran her hand through my hair as she held me.

"You okay?" she asked.

"Yes. Tired, but yes."

For a moment I considered sharing The Legend, the Mall of America, news with her, but I'd seen her eyes gloss over too many times as I explained—in great detail—different wrestling storylines, how they intersected, and why they were important for the global storyline, to know better. And I could tell she didn't have the energy.

"What about you?" I asked.

"Tired," she said, smiling. "But better now that you're here. I was thinking that maybe me and you could, you know, go on a trip. I should know this, but are there any more school breaks this semester? Does that sound like fun?"

I nodded, unsure if I should ask why she was back early from the trip with Scott.

"So, what happened to the, uh, romantic yoga getaway?"

She blew air through her lips and rolled her eyes. "He told me I was distracting from his practice. So I came home. Jesus, I can't believe I just said those words out loud."

I'll practice . . . practice knockin' his candy-ass out!

"We're going to dinner when he gets back, which . . . will be good." She sighed. "Maybe it was all moving a little too quickly anyway."

She glanced at me, as if she'd said something wrong. I shook my head, an easy grace. Besides, I knew how she was going to end the sentence already. She liked him. He made her feel something other than the low-grade grief that we were wading through every day. And while I personally thought Scott and his practice could jump in cold-ass Lake Superior, I didn't say it. If that tranquil, world-music-listening yogi fool made her happy, that was enough.

"Make him take you someplace expensive," I said.

"The man only eats wheatgrass, Julie."

Candy. Ass.

I barked out a laugh and then covered my mouth, mostly out of surprise. I didn't even know what wheatgrass was, but it didn't sound like the start of a good date. As soon as that thought crossed my mind, I thought of Max and Bri.

"Hey, can I ask you something?"

"Of course, honey."

Suddenly, my lips were frozen—locked by an emotion I didn't entirely understand. I was happy for Max, I really was. But there hadn't ever been a moment when it wasn't just me and him, the benefits of being outcasts whose parents were friends. But could this change be thornier than I let on?

"So, Max and Bri are going to prom together."

Mom sat up a little straighter. "Okay. Tell me more."

"I'm happy for him. You met her. She's awesome."

"But . . ."

"I don't know that I want to share him? Even though I'm happy that I get to share him? And it makes me feel like a total creep. If that makes sense?"

Mom pulled me close and stroked my hair. I could hear her heart beating through the soft cotton of her shirt. It reminded me of when I was a little kid, falling asleep in her arms as we walked out of a movie.

"It makes sense," she said. "Because it's how I felt about your father all the time."

I sat up. I knew all their stories, every single one indexed in my body. But I'd never heard one that started this way.

"It's just, your father—" Mom sighed. "He was so damn magnetic. Everybody loved him. Everybody, Julie. Do you remember how many people were at the church for the funeral?"

The place had been packed, standing room only. Dad liked to say that a good funeral was an example of a life well-lived and by that criteria, he held the championship belt, I guess.

"I hate to admit it, but for a long time I was jealous. Of everybody. Not that I thought your dad was—I don't know—stepping out on me."

"Wow. 'Stepping out.' I feel like we're in an episode of *Leave It to Beaver* or something."

"You know what I mean, Julie. I'm trying to tell you that the good people in our lives will always be people we have to share, mostly because that's why they're good. They just . . . treat people a little better and see things a little differently."

This was both a story I'd never heard and one that I knew at a bone level. Something about my father crossed all borders—no matter how a person might've known him. A good person. A solid dude. The type of guy who would do anything for you.

"So, what do I do?" I asked.

Mom thought about this for a second and then said, "Enjoy him. Okay? Just enjoy him."

We spent the rest of the night grumbling together about Scott and men in general, even though I admit to not having the résumé for too much vitriol. Still, it seemed to help Mom, and early Sunday morning I woke up to the sound of a chair scraping against the hardwood floors. It was early. The sky was a mist gray, enough for me to know that I was owed at least another hour of sleep. But the longer I stayed in bed, the more my eyes seemed to open.

Eventually I gave in and got up, stumbling to the kitchen. Mom was hanging party streamers, which made me think I was perhaps sleepwalking.

"What are you doing?"

"We're having a 'Scott is a dick' party this afternoon," she said plainly, raising the streamer and eyeing it to make sure it was level. "I was texting with Kathy last night. She and Greg are coming over—I think Max and Bri. too."

She turned around, remembering our conversation last night.

"Oh, Julie. Is that going to be okay with you?"

I nodded. Even if it wasn't, I was too tired to care about it right now.

"Where did you get all of this?" I asked, motioning to boxes of decorations that I'm pretty sure were actually for bachelorette parties. There were dicks everywhere.

"Same-day delivery," Mom said. "Online shopping isn't all bad, I guess. "

And listen, I appreciated the commitment to the bit. But I was tired of taping them to the walls of our house about five minutes later, not to mention by the time I heard Kathy's familiar, high-pitched, upper-Midwest voice ring out.

Before I could even say hello, Kathy was mixing orange juice and prosecco, pouring one for Mom and then one for herself. Kathy was giving Mom relationship advice, how she should strike first—"Dump his ass. Even if he is sexy. This shit doesn't fly."

I tried to block all of it out.

I could recite one of my classic Hell or Highwater promos as a distraction.

Ahem.

"Julie—what's the boy situation at Central?"

"You like to think that you're talking to God. . . ."

Kathy drained her glass and stood up to make another one, still waiting for me to answer. It reminded me of the time one of Max's aunts—hair piled on top of her head like a party trick—had cornered me and asked me about my intentions with Max, to which I responded that we planned on watching Adrenaline and maybe ordering a pizza, which she took as some kind of euphemism and tried to get my visitation rights revoked. But Kathy and Greg knew better. Still, I pretended I didn't hear Kathy.

"You like to think that God is listening. . . ."

"Julie—Kathy asked you a question."

"There is no situation," I said. "I really don't talk to any boys except Max."

"But it isn't God who's listening. . . ."

"What about this Bri girl?" Kathy said, smiling at me. "Do you like her?"

"Yes. She's great."

"Well, she seems to have totally wooed Max's skinny ass."

"Speaking of skinny asses," Mom said. "Scott told me that one of his yoga goals this year was to really focus on his gluteral intentions."

"No, when you're alone at night and you think you're talking to God . . . it's me."

Kathy and Mom roared with laughter, clinking together their glasses and sloshing mimosas on the table. As Mom went to find a towel, Kathy stood up and retrieved a wayward streamer. She lifted it so it matched the other end near the door. Once it was re-taped, she came over and gave me a hug.

"How we doing, Julie? You okay?"

"Question of my life," I deadpanned.

"Well, it's because we all love you," she said without a hint of sarcasm.

"I . . . know."

She squeezed me again. "Your mom is really going through it right now—did you know that?"

I nodded, but maybe I didn't. I had always assumed that her grief had faded, that she had somehow lost track of it, let it slip away like some negligent owner. But when did I see this? Was it me just projecting? Still, hearing that she wasn't okay hurt more than I expected.

"What can I do?" I asked.

Kathy shrugged. "Just be you. Welllll. Maybe not all you. You're a little too much like your father sometimes."

"Jesus, Kathy. Tell me how you really feel."

She laughed and leaned close, whispering into my ear. "It's why they loved each other so much. But right now, she needs you to understand that she's been trying so, so, so hard. And she went out on a limb that might've been really weak, Julie. You understand?"

I didn't want Mom to come back and see me crying so

when she came back with a towel I gave Kathy a hug and hid my face in her shoulder. Kathy gave me a final squeeze and went to help Mom. I walked outside, letting the cold air dry the last of my tears—letting the cold numb the rest of the feeling out of my body.

Max showed up a few hours later with his dad and Bri. By that time Mom and Kathy had dried out enough that they were, for the most part, just lightly giggling at everything. However, as soon as Max walked into the room he groaned.

"Oh God, what's with all the penises?"

Maybe it was Bri's presence, but Kathy and Mom both looked momentarily embarrassed. Kathy held her arms out and Max reluctantly went over, gave his mom a kiss, and then gave me a questioning look—a look that said *But seriously, can somebody explain the penises?*

Greg came over to me and gave me a peck on the cheek and said, "How are you, kiddo?"

"Good," I said.

"And you know Bri."

"They know each other, Dad," Max said.

"I set them up," I said.

Max lit up. "Oh! Like the Matchmaker!"

I groaned.

The Matchmaker was a gimmick that lasted, maybe, two weeks, where this wrestler would pull two different people out of the crowd and send them on a blind date—checking in on them throughout the episode. It was . . . uneventful, to say the least. But then on one episode, they cut to the table and . . . the couple wasn't there. They cut back to the Matchmaker, who wasn't exactly a pro on the mic and was obviously flummoxed. Back to the table and you saw the couple, hurriedly tucking in shirts and straightening bangs, fixing makeup. I didn't understand it then, but it was enough to make Dad clear his throat and get listed in the top five infamous moments in professional wrestling history.

And it was a stupid gimmick—match this, candy-ass!

Kathy gave Greg a big kiss and picked up a wineglass, tapping one of her nails on it.

"Well, an appropriate start to this lowly affair," she said. "We are here to sully the name of one Scott. Yoga doer. Tight pants enthusiast. Douche of the fourth degree."

"Oh wow, that's really saying something," Greg said, leaning over to me.

"Not only did he invite a fine woman to the North Shore for what, presumably, was a weekend of consummation and—"

"Mom!" Max said.

Kathy, there are children present!

"—excellent food, wine, and, whatever . . . yoga. But also a weekend away from her child! That means something, Scott!"

I tried not to be offended, especially because Kathy was really working herself up into a lather—making us all laugh. But I could see that Mom was also sad. Whatever she had expected of Scott—perhaps from Scott—it wasn't this. Even if it had been moving too fast, being sent home had hurt her. I walked over and put my arms around her and held on until Kathy finished.

"And so, as we lift our drinks—Greg, hand out the drinks!" Greg hurriedly handed each of us a glass with the tiniest swallow of pink wine—"we lift them to the gods of wheatgrass and yoga. May they come back and bite Scott in his diminutive, yoga-shorts-wearing, ill-formed, non-intentioned ass."

Amen!

We clinked glasses. The wine was both sweet and sour when it went down my throat. A burning I wasn't sure I enjoyed.

Mom, Kathy, and Greg were having a conversation at the table that didn't look as fun as the way the party opened. They leaned close to Mom, alternating hands on her leg, her shoulder. At one point I heard Greg tell her that she deserved better—that she deserved Dad. I couldn't watch as she buried her head into her hands and cried.

Bri had been unusually muted. When she was invited to a party at my house, she probably didn't expect all of . . . this.

Fun at parties!

"You doing okay?" I asked, surprising myself at how easily those same words slipped from my lips. I wanted to spit them out, or maybe chew them up and reconstitute them into something that actually meant something.

Bri nodded. "I just feel weird, I guess. Like I shouldn't be here. Am I intruding?"

"No," I said, sitting next to her, Max flanking her on the other side. I thought about putting my arm around her—the emotions were flying everywhere else, after all—but it felt like a bit much. Instead, I leaned close and told her, "I wouldn't want to be illegally served by Max's parents with anyone else."

"Okay, that was meant to be a sweet thing and you know it," Max said.

"Oh, I get it," I said. "I'm just wondering if the district attorney will be as understanding."

It broke whatever ice was holding Bri in place. She put one hand on my leg and one on Max's and held them there just long enough to steady herself. To smile and say, "Thank you." Behind us, Kathy started making dinner—homemade macaroni and cheese, which felt pointed given Scott's diet—and the entire house slowly began to fill up with the smell of pasta, sautéed broccoli rabe, freshly baked bread.

"So, this skater kid, Leg," Bri said. "He's got some kind of weird prom fetish or something."

"Leg is hilarious," Max said, and it came out way too excited. Bri stared at him until he dampened his enthusiasm. "But, yeah, he definitely shouldn't be on the committee. *Top Gun* prom? C'mon."

I came off the top rope to save him.

"Bri?" I said. "These guys seem barely able to make it to

their classes, let alone a not-so-hostile takeover of the prom committee."

What I didn't want to say was: I liked them. And maybe Bri could tell, because when she looked at me with suspicion, I decided it was time to ask Kathy if she needed help with dinner, which she didn't, so I cleared my throat and offered a weak, "Yeah, *Top Gun* prom. Dumb."

"Well, we need to form a voting bloc. Outvote them no matter what happens at the meeting Wednesday. Agreed?"

I hesitated, only a second, and Bri wasn't having the treason. "Max has already agreed."

Max, what a backbone you have.

"So . . . allow them on the committee but . . . don't let them have any effect on the prom. That doesn't sound like something Wentz would approve of."

Bri bobbed her head from side to side, as if she was navigating the thin line between morality and getting what she wanted. "It's definitely a gray area. But I'm trying to preserve our class's legacy, Julie."

I laughed, but Bri was actually serious, which only made me laugh harder.

Dinner was one of the more wonderful meals I'd ever eaten. There was something powerful about allowing yourself to be taken care of, Dad told me once when I didn't want him bandaging . . . something. I couldn't even remember what now. How funny. But once the bleeding had stopped, he told me about an aunt who had left him some money in a will, a nothing amount when it was all said and done, which he'd used to fund a surfing trip to Hawaii years before. But when he told me the story, he could barely get through it without getting choked up.

"It matters when people choose to take care of you, Juliana. When they want to make sure you're going to be taken care of later on. That matters in a big way."

I don't know that I really understood it until tonight, until I saw how completely Greg and Kathy cared for Mom. We hadn't seen them in a while, maybe it had even been months. They could've just shaken their heads—*That poor woman*—and chalked it up to another sad moment for a sad family. Instead, it was homemade macaroni and cheese and setting up a board game that they were now pretending to play, if only to give Mom something to focus on for the next hour.

Me, Max, and Bri ate on the couch, rewatching the episode of Adrenaline and trying to explain the importance of The Legend's return to Bri, who literally couldn't care less.

"But he's so old," she said. "Don't they have younger wrestlers?"

"That's what makes it fun," Max explained. "It's a comeback."

Don't call it a comeback!

"Wrestling fans are suckers for this kind of stuff," I added.

"Right, but, like, isn't he going to get hurt? He's really old."

Max paused. Looked at me, slightly incredulously—or

perhaps wondering if he needed to break the truth to Bri. He finally lowered his voice and said, "You know it's fake, right, Bri?"

She hit him, hard. "Yeah, I'm not an idiot. And he's still really old."

Max sat back on the couch and shook his head. "I can't with this—you talk to her."

"It's just—wrestling loves a good story. And The Legend coming back is about as good of a story as you can get. It makes you wonder what's going to happen next. And for those few seconds, hours—maybe you get a couple of days—you get to believe again."

Well said, Juliana. Well said.

CHAPTER THIRTEEN

The next few days went by impossibly fast, like a heat-seeking missile dodging class after class, headed straight for the strange collection of people who have either signed up or been forced against their will to gather after school for any number of strange, home-grown clubs and activities. Anything from robotics to anime to people who cared about prom.

When I walked into the room after school on Wednesday, the three tables were arranged into a U shape, with Bri and Max on one side of the table, Margo and Penelope on another, and Leg and God on the third. It was as tense as a global peace summit, nobody talking, all of them staring across the table with various levels of annoyance. I got the sense that Leg and God were playing this up more than the others. I couldn't stop myself.

"Oh, I'm sorry, this looks like prom stuff," I said. "I was looking for the *Top Gun* appreciation club."

Bri gave me a dirty look, but it made Leg perk up a little bit. He kicked a chair out next to him. God shook his head and tried to stifle his laughter.

"No, uh-uh. She's sitting on this side," Bri said, standing up and pulling out a chair next to her and Max. I walked over, pulled out a chair, and sat in the middle of the U.

"Switzerland," I said, sitting down.

Bri didn't look mad, just disappointed, and Max was working hard to hide his smile. After she finished processing my betrayal, Bri cleared her throat and trained her eyes on the two boys sitting across from her.

"Okay, let's not waste any more time," Bri said. "*Top Gun* prom. Stupid? Yes. But I'm fair, so let's vote and get this over with."

"Well, I've prepared an opening statement, if you'd entertain me," Leg said, looking at me and smiling.

Bri sighed for a really long time, before giving him a curt "Sure."

Leg stood, clearing his throat. God smoothed the wrinkles on Leg's T-shirt before saying, "You look great, dear. Knock them dead."

"So . . . enchanted gardens. Pretty terrible prom theme, amirite?"

Bri's patience was spent instantly. She cut in with an explanation of how she, Margo, and Penelope had researched classic prom themes throughout the decades and that enchanted gardens allowed them to both honor the past and put a new spin on it for the modern-day prom goer.

"So, it's both historic and elegant."

"And it's a total snoozefest," Leg said. God elbowed him

and Leg bit his lip. "Listen, prom is important to all of us in this room, right?"

I looked down at the table. I really didn't care about prom. I could feel Leg's eyes on me, his smile creeping up my neck like two fingers—slowly tickling my skin until I raised my head and smiled back at him. Bri looked at me incredulously.

Juliana, I think I *am a fan of prom.*

"I'm, uh, listening," I said, clearing my throat.

"Yeah, prom is important," Bri said. "That's why I'm not going to let you ruin it."

"I'm not trying to ruin it!" Leg said.

Bri looked like she was about to separate Leg's head from his body, so I spoke up. "I think we started this meeting wrong. We probably should've started with introductions. Or an icebreaker."

Everybody stared at me like I was the one whose head had just rolled across the floor.

Max, ever the conflict avoider, picked up what I was putting down. "Yeah, okay, I'm Max and I'm kind of like a crisis actor, just your standard designated vote for everything that my girlfriend tells me to vote for."

Bri's eyes could've killed him, and I wouldn't be surprised if he lost an appendage with the way she was squeezing his arm. I was pretty sure he was joking. Max wouldn't look at me, maybe because he had used a word neither of us had ever heard him use before—"girlfriend."

Still, it worked.

"Penelope. And I have no idea what is happening."

"Margo. And I don't care."

"Well, I'm Leg and I'm here to stop the steal!" Leg said without a hint of sarcasm. "And this is my friend God, who cares deeply about prom."

"'Deeply' would be a vast overstatement," God said. "But I am definitely invested in the potential *unraveling* of society that would come with a *Top Gun*–themed prom."

When it was my turn I waved and said, "I'm Julie, still looking for that cool nickname, so hit me up with your ideas, God and Leg. Anyway, I'm here because I'm hoping to be betrothed by the end of all this. It just makes life easier if you get things locked up early. You know."

There was an awkward silence before Leg laughed, loudly, and Bri stared at me like, *What in the hell are you doing?*

I'm here to introduce you to a new kind of chaos—get some, jabronis!

"Okay, thank you, Julie?" Bri said. "Anyway, I'm Bri and I want to remind everyone that people are excited about enchanted gardens because, like I said before, it has the qualities all good prom themes have."

"Foliage?" Leg asked.

"*Magic* foliage," God said. He snapped his fingers. "Oh! Magic foliage. I vote for that."

Bri looked totally flustered, which made me feel bad for her. She closed her eyes and settled herself.

"Can you . . . just tell us why you want to change it to *Top Gun* and then we can vote?"

Leg looked at God, who gave him two thumbs-up.

"Because it's awesome," Leg said.

"Seriously? That's your pitch."

"Uh, yeah?" Leg looked completely confused, as if he'd ended the conversation with those three words.

"It is kind of awesome," Max said, which made Leg point at him.

"I know, right?"

Bri turned to Max, who quickly added, "But our prom theme, uh, can't be a joke."

"That's right," Bri said. "It needs to be something that, twenty years from now, we can look back and be proud of."

"Counterpoint: if I care about the prom theme in my late thirties, somebody needs to punch me right in the nuts," Leg said. He turned to God and said, "Seriously, I give you permission, dude, okay?"

God smiled, almost unnoticeably. Leg turned to Bri, then me. He seemed to understand that Max was going whichever way Bri pointed.

"Margo? Penelope? Thoughts?"

Both Penelope and Margot glanced up from their phones, completely checked out of the conversation. They shared a look and Margo shrugged.

"Listen, I know you think I'm just here to screw around," Leg said. "But I actually care about this."

"He's not lying," God said. "He is a prom truther, for reasons that are completely incomprehensible."

"Think about it." Leg stood up and started pacing back

and forth on his side of the table like a trial attorney. Bri was unmoved. "Twenty years from now, is 'enchanted gardens' going to be any different than, say, 'making memories' or 'a night to remember'?"

"Don't forget 'magic foliage,'" God said, kicking his feet onto the table as he opened a bag of Funyons.

"Right, another good example, thank you, my man."

God raised a Funyon.

"But *Top Gun*? I know you think it's ridiculous—and it is! But that's what makes it so amazing. There's no way that doesn't go viral. And when we look back in twenty years—at the very least you'll chuckle. You're going to remember that theme for the rest of your life."

Talk to me, Goose!

Bri started to talk but stopped herself. So Leg powered forward. "Let's put it to a vote—if it fails, fine. Whatever. I'll drop it. But know that I'm not just here trying to cause chaos. At least acknowledge that much."

Bri sighed again and reluctantly said, "Okay, well, all in favor of a *Top Gun*–themed prom raise your hand."

Leg's and God's hands shot up. In a move that can only be described as sacrificial—was Bri the highwater mark of Max's dating life?—Max raised his hand while simultaneously offering an apology to Bri, who looked absolutely shocked by how quickly this had turned.

"Okay, I'm going to assume that the Bri and the two Holy Roller—sorry, Holy Angels—members are pro-enchanted gardens soooo . . . ," Leg said.

Leg and Bri both turned to me. Bri shook her head.

"Don't you do it, Julie. . . ."

I wanted to be on the right side of history, so I raised my hand, too.

Because, *Top Gun* prom.

Bri wouldn't talk to me or Max until we were in the parking lot and then all she could manage was, "I can't!" By the time we got to her car, Max must've started worrying she was really mad because he leaned in and said something that made her laugh. She pushed him away, still laughing, and when he came back in close, they kissed.

"Well, that's my cue," I said, heading to the sidewalk.

"Don't you want a ride?" Max asked.

It was warm, the first signs of actual spring in Minnesota. Holding you hostage in the morning and then creating Stockholm Syndrome in the afternoon with the bare minimum of what can be considered "nice" weather.

"I kind of want to walk," I said. "No big deal. I'll see you all later."

I started walking down Marshall Avenue, toward my house in theory but with no actual urgency to get home. As I walked, the buildings slowly changed from residential to the athletic fields of a small college and then to industrial. Ahead, beneath an overpass, a few guys laughed as they skated up and down a short concrete embankment. When I got closer, I saw Leg and God, with a few others. As soon as he saw me, Leg waved—both hands—and kicked himself over to me on his skateboard, jumping off and catching it in his hand as soon as he got close.

"Hey! It's Married Lady!"

"What?" I asked.

"Betrothed. I know my SAT words," Leg said. As he talked, God rode up on his skateboard. Leg looked frenetic when he rode, an exposed wire, whereas God seemed to ride with a calmness that was incongruent with his speed.

"Hey, Julie."

"You live around here?" Leg asked. "We live over that way."

Leg pointed south, toward my house. I nodded and told him we might be neighbors. His face went serious.

"Do you have a date to prom?"

"Oh Jesus," God said. "Please excuse my friend. He does not have social skills."

"What? I need a date to prom."

"First, you barely know this girl. Second, you don't need a date to prom; you want a date to prom."

This kid's got some moxie, Juliana.

Leg looked at God incredulously. "You know my situation. This is a need situation."

"Uh, what are we talking about?" I asked, more amused than anything else. Leg, excited now, spun to face me.

"If you go to prom all four years, you get a custom-made martini glass—like lettering in sports, but it's, you know, prom."

I was pretty sure this was not an actual thing. But Leg

didn't seem to be playing an angle. If anything, he was almost too earnest—too sweet for his own good, or at least for being in high school.

But I couldn't say yes, and I didn't want to say no, so instead I smiled and said, "I'm actually philosophically against prom."

"Before marriage?" Leg joked again, and I felt myself blush.

"Or after."

It's a life commitment, Leg.

"Well, it was worth a shot. I won't hold it against you," he said, dropping his board to the ground. "But I should thank you. I can't believe I actually made *Top Gun* prom happen."

"We—we made *Top Gun* prom happen," I said.

Leg looped around and gave me a high five as God chuckled, saying, "This is going to backfire on you in a major way, bro."

"What? How?"

"It's literally going to be me, my date, and you at this prom."

"Fine! Who needs a crowd? They won't be, like, checking attendance records twenty years from now."

"You really are concerned about the posterity of prom," I said.

Leg shrugged. "What can I say? I care."

"Well, there is no way Bri and Max aren't going to prom. So it won't be just you guys."

"And we'll work on getting you philosophically

pro-prom," Leg said, still circling me on his board—still smiling.

The heat started climbing into my face again. I had no idea what was happening or why Leg seemed able to say just about anything and it made me want to simultaneously run away and . . . I didn't know.

"Good luck with that," I said, and even that felt like flirting, sounded like flirting, and I'm pretty sure I was nothing but bright, hot red.

A ripe, tomato-faced jabroni queen!

Leg stopped his skateboard and watched me. "Well, I'd offer you a ride home, but I'm trying to make a good impression."

"Oh, this is the good impression?"

God laughed and pulled Leg back toward their friends. "C'mon, man, you've done enough for one day. You don't want to spoil her."

Leg mouthed, "Yes I do. . . ." and it was the corniest thing I've ever experienced, but even though I laughed, and God groaned, something inside me blew up—a shower of glittery sparks, head to toe.

It took me three times as long to get to the top of the hill, only two blocks from the underpass. I stopped, turned around, and watched them skate, listening to them lob insults at one another, each followed by rolling laughter. When I finally passed Whole Foods, out of sight, something inside me drooped—a sense of loss, maybe, or just the sudden energy change. I wanted to go running back, to grab one of their skateboards and, somehow, magically be adept. Hell, better than most of them. I could see their faces as I did a . . . jump-kick-thing. As I flipped the board underneath me like it was tied to a string. Instead, I stepped into Whole Foods and bought myself a couple of chocolate-covered pretzels. When I came back outside, I looked down the road and the boys were gone.

CHAPTER FOURTEEN

At home, Mom was sitting on the couch working on her laptop. She greeted me, distracted, and then told me we were having leftovers for dinner. I went to my room and attempted to work on my outline for my extended essay.

This will be the best homework assignment that's ever been turned in, Juliana!

People want you to know that wrestling isn't real. It's information usually followed by a laugh, one or two burps, and then some belly-button scratching while they waited for you to shake off what they assume was white-hot clarity about the world. Obviously, I've known wrestling was "fake" for half my life. Frankly, it was kind of insulting that people thought I'd be wandering around—you could say, in this case, a true danger to society—thinking that these women and men were dropping each other on their heads, shattering their spines. Somehow built different than mere mortals.

But then again, that was also kind of what was attractive about it.

It was a way to believe that the world worked differently,

that somehow, somewhere, there were giants among us, the sort of legends the world no longer thought it needed. And that said nothing of the fans, the legions of maniacs who would follow their wrestler to hell and back—people who lived, died, and bought the T-shirt.

Modern-day gladiators. A strange breed.

And then one day, they would just disappear. Sometimes you'd see it coming—you'd get the retirement tour—and other times it just happened, quicker than you can count, one-two-three-done. Emptiness where there was once greatness. Gone, but not forgotten. And all of us who were left behind—who really loved it—could do nothing but tend to the unmistakable feeling that we'd lost something important. That what remained were carbon copies, xeroxed versions of the original.

Damn, that's deep, Juliana. We should get an Orange Julius.

Mom knocked on my door, bringing me a plate of food. She looked at my computer screen, read the stream of consciousness that I was hoping, with some bullet points and a bibliography, of course, would pass as an outline.

"How's it going?" she asked gently.

"Okay," I said.

She raised an eyebrow. I could always tell when Mom was digging for information and she always seemed to know when I was holding out. Dad used to say she was about as subtle as a sledgehammer, which made sense given that she worked as a public defender. But she refused to use what he called "lawyer tricks" on either of us, refused to litigate who left the toilet seat up, again, or forgot to run the dishwasher. So, when she needed or wanted information, she'd do this—a sort of surprised tone mixed with a non-specific question.

"You sure?"

"Honestly, writing this makes me think of Dad," I said, turning to face her. "I think he would love it."

Mom smiled, and I could see her eyes welling up with tears.

"It's just . . ." She stopped herself, wiped her eyes once. "It's just . . . your dad used to talk about kayfabe all the time. How reality was never fixed—everything, for him, was changeable. It always seemed so damn depressing to me—the idea that nothing was permanent. That we all eventually just . . . what? Disappear? Ah, dammit."

She was full-on crying now. I stood up and hugged her as she sobbed quietly into my shoulder.

"He thought it was a good thing, Julie! He probably thinks it's a good thing that he's gone now! The biggest angle of all! I can hear him now!"

I had no recollection, no memory, of Dad ever saying any this, if I was being honest. However, there were moments when tragedy or crisis slid off him easier than other people. I wouldn't say that it didn't affect him, because he was also deeply empathetic—the sort of guy who would cry at the weirdest stuff, like sports podcasts. Random commercials. A total beta, as Max would jokingly say. But he wasn't soft, nor was he overly hard. More like waterproof. Things bounced off him in a way that I wish I could replicate—a way that I was increasingly unable to remember.

"I don't think he would think leaving us was a good thing," I said quietly.

She nodded then shook her head. "He was so damn infuriating sometimes. And he loved you, God did he love you."

We need some Orange Julius, Juliana—stat!

Mom wiped her eyes again. "Jesus, I'm sorry. I don't know what got into me."

I shrugged, but I knew. It was the same thing that made me hold on to every scrap of a memory I could find. The big ones, of course, but also the seemingly meaningless moments that my brain had somehow captured, tagged, and stored. Like the time we were getting gas and somebody, inexplicably, was smoking at another pump and he told me how the gas and the smoke, mixed with the cold air, reminded him of his father. Of growing up in Chicago. Or when he grumbled about how Mom and I opened bags of chips—tearing a corner off, instead of opening it from the top. He got into her, the same as me.

And now both of us were just scared that one day we'd wake up and his laugh would be a little less loud, a little less familiar in our ears. The day he would be more story, more legend, than reality.

Mom kissed me on the forehead. "Kayfabe. You are his child."

We should celebrate. At Orange Julius.

Juliana?

• • •

Max was working, of course, and I didn't feel like walking around the mall or delaying the Orange Julius fix. When I got close, Max was smiling. At least until he saw my face. He was already working on the drinks when I stepped up to the counter. He put on the finishing touches, handed one of them to me, and put the other on the counter. "You good?"

"Just been crying about kayfabe," I said.

"So . . ." Max checked his watch. "Yep, Wednesday."

Max leaned against the counter and watched the mall with me for a few minutes. Eventually he stretched and said, "So, I tried again to get us tickets to the event. I thought they might be selling employee tickets, but no. Sorry, Julie."

"I checked, too, and they were going for, like, a grand. It's all good. We'll just get the pay-per-view. And if you feel really bad, I'll let you pay. A perfect post-prom experience."

Max chuckled. "I tried to explain all of this to Bri last night."

"How did that go?" I said.

"She doesn't get it. She called it my great shame, which was kind of funny." He looked into the mall again. "It's stupid, but I thought for sure she'd, like, leave? Immediately?"

I took a sip, then a second, and said, "I hate to break it to you, Max, but that girl has lost it for you."

True love comes off the top rope, Max.

"Uh, well, I, uh, feel the same . . ."

"You should work on that before you tell her," I said, laughing.

Ring the bell, this kid is OUT!

"So, about prom . . ."

The sudden change to an all-business tone was unsettling. I looked him up and down once. ". . . Yes?"

"I'm just making sure you're, like, cool with me and Bri. You know. Going to prom."

"Max. Are you seriously saying you think I'm mad that you're not going to prom with me?"

"I mean, that's not what I was really saying," he said, blushing. "But I always just assumed that we'd go together. You know, the drought continues and such. No dates. For me. I always figured you'd marry into money."

Max looked remarkably uncomfortable, despite the joke. He kept flicking his eyes to mine. I patted his hand and took a long sip of my Orange Julius.

"C'mon. I'm happy for you," I said, and he visibly relaxed. Now it was my turn to freeze up. I took another sip of my drink. "Besides, somebody asked me."

Max dropped his phone on the counter, and I couldn't tell if it was intentional or not. His mouth was comically open. I'd probably be more pissed if he didn't look like such a clown.

"Who?"

"You don't know him. He's from Canada. We met online. He swiped right on all this."

"Whooooo?"

"I told you, international man of mystery. Canadian tuxedos. Phone apps."

Max leaned across the counter. "Know that I will maintain

eye contact with you until you tell me who this person is."

He stared at me.

He stared at me longer.

I took a long sip, froze my brain, and he kept staring.

"Fine, creep—it's Leg."

Max's eyes became saucers and he laughed, loudly. "Holy shit. No. Really?"

"He's sweet. Misguided, but sweet."

"Well, I don't think he's going to be alive long enough to take you to prom," Max said. "Bri may put a hit out on him."

"Him? I'm worried about us."

A man has to live by a code, Max. You made me proud.

Max shrugged. "Don't worry about it. I have a way about me. Nobody can stay mad for too long."

"Yeah, okay."

"I mean, I think she's essentially in the perfect spot—right? If it's a huge success, that all goes to her. If it's a huge failure, well, it wasn't her idea anyway."

I finished my Orange Julius and set the cup on the counter. "I do feel like we missed an opportunity to catch her with some misdirection and make Adrenaline-themed prom happen."

Max chuckled. "I'm pretty sure I wouldn't have a date. Or a girlfriend after that."

Of course you would, you jabroni! Women love the Adrenaline type.

"Well, I hope she doesn't hate me," I said.

And as soon as the words came out of my mouth, it was

my turn to look at Max, to wonder if I had crossed some sort of weird boundary—both of us were drawing new maps for our friendship. I wanted Bri to be a friend. I wanted her to know I had her back (except when it came to *Top Gun* prom.) When I committed, I was an oak. Max could witness to this. And now I was sitting here in the dead, closing hours of the Mall of America, wondering if I'd messed everything up.

"She doesn't hate you," Max said gently. "I mean, she was really pissed at me. But I gave her a little bit of loving and, you know . . ."

He wagged his eyebrows at me once, twice, and when I couldn't stand it anymore I pushed myself off the counter and started to walk away.

"Hey—I've got another hour left!" he yelled.

The truth was, I needed more time to think about kayfabe, which may be the only time in history somebody has thought about that exact sentence. So I walked the Mall, reversing my normal route, and thinking about what Mom had said—"He probably thought it was a good thing!"

I couldn't believe that and neither did Mom, I was certain. But it exposed something that I didn't want to acknowledge.

What if believing in kayfabe was actually bad? What if it only seeded confusion and regret? And perhaps what hurt the most: Could Dad have been wrong in this big, fundamental way?

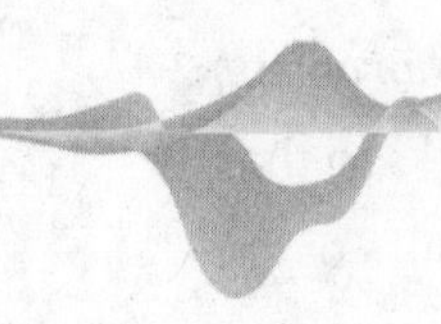

CHAPTER FIFTEEN

The next morning Leg was waiting for me at the top of the stairs, just outside of Wentz's class. He had a small can of orange soda and a plastic rose the size of a pencil. His smile was working overtime.

"For you," he said, holding out the gifts. "I didn't have time to go anywhere else, so I had to get these from Speedway."

"What is this for?" I asked.

"Courting," God said, walking up next to Leg. "His word, not mine."

"Listen, I know I threw out the whole prom thing a little casually yesterday, so this is my way of apologizing and, also, showing you that I'm serious."

I looked at the orange soda, the rose, and couldn't stop my stomach from jumping a little bit.

Look at this over-reachin', Don Juan-abee jabroni. . . .

"Well, I appreciate it," I said. "Speedway or not."

"I've seen you drinking those orange smoothies so I figured, same thing," Leg said, opening up the can of soda and handing it to me.

Orange smoothies!

"The rose was, uh . . ." Leg searched for the word.

"Inspiration," God said, chuckling.

"Yeah, something like that," Leg said. His entire mood changed almost instantly. Gone was the brash kid on the skateboard. Instead, Leg was a shuffling, nervous mess. As soon as the bell rang, he said, "Right, see ya," and then bolted down the staircase.

"Wow, that was a case study in how not to do it," God said, getting ready to follow his friend. But then he stopped and faced me. "He's a good dude, just so you know. And this is him, like, really trying. Okay?"

And then he was gone.

Wentz completely lost his shit when he read my outline, nodding and making these low guttural noises every time he came across something that resonated. When he finished, he handed the outline back to me and smiled—big.

"Julie, this is exceptional work. It's well-written, insightful—even vulnerable, which isn't a requirement for the project but is the sort of thing that makes me think you're uncovering something with this. What do you think?"

"I think I'm going through an existential crisis," I said.

"Well, that's normal for an extended essay."

I stared at him. "Are you serious? Existential dread is a learning goal?"

He smiled and said, "Well, not exactly. But now is the time to dig deeper—see where the joy takes you."

Where the Joy Takes You was the name of the Breathtaking One's second self-help book, and maybe Wentz realized his gaffe because he put my paper down and said, "I will take wrestling at any time, even if it's self-help."

"He's coming to the Mall. Max and I are going to the signing. I'm going to talk trash to him."

Wentz paused. "Well, that seems . . . very you, Julie."

After that, Wentz gave us the rest of the period to work on the opening pages of our essays. He turned on a playlist, just loud enough that its murmur could be heard by everyone in the room but not beyond. All around me, people got to work—typing on iPads, scribbling notes into their notebooks. A few people were rearranging note cards on their desk. I looked at the piece of paper Wentz handed back to me and the words looked foreign—perhaps even seditious.

If kayfabe wasn't real, what was I doing with myself?

Wrestling, for me at least, had always been a source of vulnerability. I didn't go around asking people to list their favorite mid-continental champions or anything. And while that list, of course, started with the Nashville Stud, I also wasn't sure it should be the sole basis of my personality.

One of the gifts of professional wrestling was its ability to mimic, even taunt, reality. And there were plenty of people who perhaps believed in reality too much. Dad liked to say that those people believed they had all the answers . . . until they didn't.

The Masked Man wasn't always the Masked Man. In fact he bounced around different promotions for the first part of his career, adopting any number of terrible personas, including the Man from Planet X, the Cat Burglar, one-half of the tag team Pain and Suffering, and Mr. Awful. Always with a mask, of course, but at first he was meant to be a jobber, a person who existed only to make other wrestlers popular. So naturally people hated him, which eventually grew to becoming the wrestler that everybody loved to hate, which finally transformed into simple love.

They wanted a jobber; they got a man of the people.

That was real. It wasn't manufactured in some writer's room, a trick to make you believe. It developed and became real because people loved him, the gimmick—the mask.

Was that kayfabe or not?

The bell rang and I ran to the front of the room, slapping my paper down on Wentz's desk. He took a second to read what I've written.

"So . . . the benefits of sometimes, maybe, breaking kayfabe?" He nodded and then looked up at me. "I like it, Julie. A lot. Are you . . . okay with this?"

I didn't want to think about what it meant. In fact, if I could simply phone the essay in, I would've done so already. Now, of course, I would have to deal with the fact that I had not only created extra work for myself by completely rethinking my thesis while also simultaneously becoming an extended essay cliché. Most people wrote about some pedestrian topic, basically a history paper. Twenty-five, crisply typed, with no introspection whatsoever. But the research was always—always!—followed by a sort of confessional, saccharine-sweet wrap-up of "the high school experience."

What is high school, if not a field for growing memories?

Gross.

And here I was, trying to shake the foundations of what little life I had. I sighed.

"We'll see."

When I saw Max and Bri at lunch, they'd picked up a straggler—Leg. He was talking animatedly, and when they came into earshot I heard him say, "I'm essentially copresident, though, right? I mean, I think that's only fair. Title bump? For the résumé?"

Bri looked absolutely dumbstruck when Leg sat down at our table, as natural as if he'd been a part of our friend group from the start. How had her life taken such a right turn? She looked at me for help.

"What about *wingman*?" I asked.

Leg's face lit up and Bri gave me a look that would spoil milk. But behind it, I could tell that she had already accepted that *Top Gun* prom was happening, and perhaps even that Leg was now a part of her life—if only for a couple more weeks.

He only looks like a candy-ass, haha!

From across the cafeteria, God whistled. Leg jumped up and grabbed his backpack and skateboard.

"Well, duty calls," he said, pronouncing it "doody," which made me laugh. Max and Bri stared at me like I'd lost my damn mind.

"Don't hurt yourself," Bri said dryly.

"Maybe I need a wingman," Leg said over his shoulder. "Max, think about it, my man!"

Oh yeahhhhh! Tag team of the century!

"I should go skate with them sometime," Max said.

The idea of Max hanging out with Leg, God, and the rest of the road-rashed skaters was something I couldn't really comprehend. Max, the consummate button-up—Mr. Responsible. The sort of person you could take to meet your mother, day one. And then Leg who was . . . not that.

"That would be amazing," I said. "You could bring that little board you got in, what, fifth grade?"

"The Ripper. Hell, yeah."

"Didn't that thing come with, like, handlebars?" I asked.

Max did a double take, like I'd slapped him not once, but twice. The Ripper was the sort of skateboard a kid could grow into, not that it wasn't styled with a sick purple, black, and neon yellow color scheme—like bottled lighting. I couldn't lie; I was jealous as hell when he got it. He came riding by my house all casual, like, "Yeah, I ride a Ripper." I'd sit in my front window, Ripper-less. A sad sack.

"It didn't have handlebars. Jesus, Julie."

Max looked at Bri, who was completely lost. A skateboard with handlebars. As if, right?

Haha!

But trust me, it had handlebars. It was marketed to moms, certainly, as the first step to letting your kid become a true Ripper delinquent. A Ripper-lite, scooter version—complete with easy steering! And hey, maybe your kid wasn't going to end up being Ripper material. Maybe they would really jive with that handlebar. Become a scooter king.

Scooter King!

"It legit was a scooter, Max."

"You had to literally bolt the . . ." Max stopped, searching for a word other than *handlebar.* When he couldn't find one, he said, "Well, it was marketed as a skateboard. So that settles it."

I turned to Bri confidentially. "He just took the handlebars off last year. When he got his license."

"I need new friends," Max said

"I bet you could start a scooter club," Bri said.

I was laughing when the PA speakers crackled to life. It was weird how conditioned we'd become, because everybody stopped moving, talking, everything—the entire cafeteria. Principal Macabee's patient voice came across the speakers.

"Greetings, Central Family, I wanted to update you on a big, exciting decision."

Macabee was about the most no-nonsense person you would meet. Grown-ass boy-men, fighting in the hallways and talking shit, would stop dead when they saw her clopping down the hallway in her heels, calling every student by name. Every single one of them.

However, when she continued, there was a certain weariness to her words. My ears perked up a little more when she said, "So now it's my . . . great pleasure . . . to turn the microphone over to Mr. Francis Root for an announcement about prom."

Just off mic I heard Leg's voice say, "It's Leg." But Principal Macabee didn't say anything else, and suddenly Leg's voice came across the speakers.

"Uh, hey, it's Leg and I'm, uh, copresident of the prom committee . . ."

There was a long pause. A really, really long pause.

"Yeah, so, I'm coming to you LIVE . . ." Leg seemed to catch his stride here and, even though it was like going from zero to a thousand in one word, it worked. He was rolling. "That's right, CENTRAL. Coming at you LIVE from the office of Principal Macabee . . ."

"Get to it, Francis," Macabee said, just off mic.

"Right, well, I know you thought you were going to spend prom stumbling around some kind of enchanted garden, right?"

There was one half-hearted "woo" from the crowded cafeteria. I looked over at Bri, who seemed to be taking all of this as well as could possibly be expected. Max put an arm around her shoulder.

"Well, I'm here to tell you that the MAVERICKS on the prom committee just made things a little more . . . dangerous." There was another pause, this time intentionally, as Leg cued up the Kenny Loggins's song "Danger Zone," made famous in the movie *Top Gun.* At first, nobody was sure what to do—because what the hell was happening?

"That's right. This year's prom theme has been changed!" Leg was literally breathless with excitement, as if he was dancing. I wanted to peek around the corner and look into the office, just to catch a glimpse of him. But if I did that, I would never hear the end of it from Max, so I sat there and listened as he finally said, "*TOP GUN* PROM. Best night of your life? You better damn well believe it."

I heard Macabee say, "Okay . . ."

There was a brief struggle for the microphone and, once again off mic, Leg yelled, "I'm Leg, copresident—no, WINGMAN—of the prom committee, and I approve this message!"

And just before the mic cut out, God said: "'Talk to me, Goose!'"

I looked over at Bri, half expecting her to be freaking out. If anything, she seemed resolved.

"God help us," she said.

Top Gun prom was an immediate hit in the hallways, the classrooms—even with the teachers, who were always ready for some nostalgia. Yeah, of course, a lot of people didn't know the movie, and for sure hadn't seen it. Probably not even the more recent sequel. But it didn't stop the mania from sweeping through the entirety of the school like a capsizing wave. I half expected to see somebody wearing a flight suit by the end of the day, but instead it was just Leg—now the most popular kid in the whole school based on the way people were slapping his shoulder and shouting out his name—wearing a pair of cheap, gas station aviator sunglasses.

"Popularity is fleeting," he said, popping a Cheeto into

his mouth. "I do my work for the people."

"Well, at least you've solved your prom date problem," God said. "Take your pick, bro."

My stomach tightened as a girl walked by and said hello to Leg. I felt like I was blinking too much—was I blinking too much?—but neither Leg or God seemed to notice so I stood there, trying not to stare or read into how he grunted and shrugged away all the attention.

"More importantly," God said. "Where are we skating tonight?"

Leg licked the Cheeto dust off his thumb and then lifted it in the air, as if he were checking the wind. I'm pretty sure this had nothing to do with skating but was some sort of extended bit between him and God. But he committed to it, pulling the sunglasses down on his nose and squinting an eye into the gray afternoon sky.

"Let's go the Lair," he said. "My trick knee says it's going to snow."

"Well, my weather app does not, but you know I'm down," God said. He then turned to me and said, "You wanna tag along?"

"Skating? No. God no. I'm sorry. But that would be bad."

I was definitely talking too much and both Leg and God were immediately attuned to my discomfort. And Leg, at least, was amused.

"So . . . you're saying you're *not* interested?"

This kid.

It made me laugh, which released the tension—whatever

butterflies had been swimming in my stomach the last few days. And in that moment, I was trying to will Leg to ask me to prom again, right then on the steps of Central. Crowds be damned. Because for some reason every lick of sense I had, every defense I'd built up, was either gone or down and I might've just said yes—even though I hadn't "just said yes" to anything in longer than I could remember. There was no script.

Do it, you candy-ass, or I'll hit you with the sleeper hold and then it's good night!

For a second I thought it worked. Leg stared at me, not blinking, and God, to his credit, cleared his throat and took a few steps away from us.

"Uh, maybe I could get your number?" Leg said. "Text you sometime. Maybe walk by your house a hundred times hoping you notice me. I don't just skate, you know."

"Yes, he does!" God said, obviously still able to hear us. "But give him your phone number, Julie."

Give the candy-ass your number, Juliana. You deserve it.

I was about to ask him for his phone, but he handed me his skateboard instead and said, "Write it here. I lose my phone all the time."

So I wrote my number on the side of his skateboard, which tightened my stomach once again. That wonderful sickness that didn't leave even when he and God went sliding down the long railing of the staircase and then skating down the sidewalk, leaving me alone in the crowd in front of the school. Stomach still fluttering.

CHAPTER SIXTEEN

When I got home, something was wrong. The lights were off and the shades pulled. I didn't see Mom at first. I was standing there with the door open, letting the light in, when she called my name.

"Close the door, honey. Please."

She was on the couch, under a pile of blankets. I closed the door and walked up the stairs quietly, intent on not making noise—was it a migraine? But when I came up next to her, I saw the bloodshot eyes. The tissues. The obvious signs of a person who hadn't been able to stop themselves from crying.

"What happened?" I asked.

"I'm stupid," she says. "So stupid."

Somebody is about to catch an ass-whuppin'.

I looked around the room for a clue. Mom wasn't exactly dramatic. Even when Dad died, she'd had the remarkable ability to keep it together when I was falling apart. It didn't mean that she didn't cry or grieve. And when you were hurting—when you needed a mom because you no longer had a dad—it was the best sacrifice a parent could make. She showed up. She kept showing up and holding me, refusing to let me go until I'd cried every tear my body could manage. And knowing there would be more—there were always more—she never got annoyed, never told me to get over it or to buck up buttercup, just sat with me and sat with me some more.

"Scott," she said. "God, this is stupid. I went to see him and I thought we were going to fix it and—"

She couldn't get the next words out.

"What? What happened?"

"He broke up with me."

That linen shirt-wearing, wheatgrass-eatin', about-to-have-my-boot-in-his-ass jabroni? Let me get a "Hell no!"

Hell. No.

I sat down next to her and put my arm around her. She leaned into me.

"He wasn't ready for 'a commitment.'"

Are you ready to whoop some ass, Juliana? To Whoop. Some. Candy. Ass?

"Well, that's what you call a dick move, Mom."

"Julie!"

"What? The guy's obviously a dick."

Stupid-lookin', candy-ass-havin'. . . .

"He was nice to me," she said quietly. "Even though the retreat was a disaster, I . . . really thought . . ."

I paused. It had been nice to see Mom happy—I wanted Mom to be happy. But Scott, with his smiles, vague zen practice, all that talk of oneness . . . well, it made me feel like the parent. The one who could see beyond the present circumstance, who always knew that eventually Scott wasn't going to be in our lives anymore.

For a moment I panicked. I didn't want to admit that there would be a day when someone would stick around, when it would happen for Mom and even for me. The moment when we could let Dad go, if only long enough to move forward a few more steps.

But not for this candy-ass jabroni.

"I'm sorry, Mom. I really am."

This made her start crying all over again, and I held her until she finally sat up, wiped her eyes, and groaned.

"God. I am not doing this for Scott," she said. "I'm just not. I don't think I even cried when your father broke up with me."

"Wait. What?" How many more stories had I not heard?

Mom looked at me, confused. "Your dad broke up with me in college once. You know this story."

"Uh . . . the only story I know is how you and Dad had this storybook romance that I'll never be able to compete with, including four years of college antics that I'm still Not Old Enough to Know About."

"Well, it isn't much of a story," she said. "Your father broke up with me because . . . hell, I still don't know why, honestly. Anyway, it came out of nowhere and it really pissed me off, so I was, like, 'See ya!' Didn't cry a single tear for that jerk."

"This is scandalous, Mom."

"Not really. I mean, we were back together a week later.

He saw me out on a date with Jonathan Gallagher and about lost it."

"Mom. There is no shame in your game."

"Thanks, honey. That means a lot coming from you." Mom kissed me on the cheek and stretched her arms over her head. "Okay, I'm tired of this boo-hoo routine. I want to do something fun."

"Maybe you could look up Jonathan Gallagher's phone number."

Mom laughed. "Jonathan is a Roman Catholic priest. So . . . maybe not that scandalous. Besides, I think I have a better idea."

Mom told me to pack a bag and, meanwhile, she ran around the house throwing things into a suitcase like the world was ending and we had tickets on the only ship off the planet. And I'd probably be more worried that Mom was having some sort of break with reality if she wasn't narrating the entire plan—perhaps as it came to her—in real time.

"We'll go up to Grand Marais, the North Shore. No yoga! Just eating all the fried food and drinking all the wine—well, me, not you—that I want. I'm looking at you, Scott!"

Your mom is an ass-kicking machine, Juliana.

"How long are we going to be gone?" I asked, making Mom pause for a second. She shrugged. "Because, you know, school?"

"Oh, I'll call you in. Let's say—three days? So, you'll only miss tomorrow."

And then she was back to circling the house like a banshee, talking her own brand of trash to a nonexistent Scott.

"I might even buy us some non-free-trade chocolate to eat on the road, SCOTT."

"Stick this up your ASS chakra, SCOTT."

"I hope your hairline recedes . . . MORE!"

And so on.

I finished packing and sat on the couch, listening to Mom's continued rant ("You dress like a cut-rate wizard, SCOTT.")

I pulled out my phone to create a group text with me, Bri, and Max.

Me: So my mom is losing her shit a bit. Scott breakup

Max: Oh. Well. Scott was a douche so

Me: This was alluded to. We're going up north for a few days. I wanted to let you know I didn't get taken

Bri: I have a certain set of skills, Julie

Me: . . . none of which would help me if I got taken

Bri: Harsh

Max: Hey maybe you would call Leg . . .

Me: I was going to say "sorry" for missing adrenaline again but now I'm signing off. Max, never text me again

In the car, driving north, the cracks in Mom's forced optimism—her rage—started to show. Streaks of tears became visible as cars passed us on the highway. I tried to distract her with questions about the cabin.

Mom handed me her phone. "It's a 'cozy getaway'

according to the description. We're lucky to have gotten it last second like this. It says it's almost never available."

I flipped through the pictures of what looked to be a cute apartment that claimed it was steps away from Lake Superior, filled with "charm" and "quirkiness."

"Can we go to that place we went when I was a kid?" I asked.

"Ben Franklin's? Yeah, of course. That sounds like fun."

I leaned back in the seat and took a deep breath. Sometimes I thought I could still smell Dad in the car, which was impossible since Mom got it detailed every spring—something Dad eternally gave her shit about. Bourgeois, he called it. And she would fire back about his truck—now mine—smelling like an armpit, which wasn't very far off. But even these days it smelled more like my armpit than his.

A few snowflakes were falling as we drove, slowly becoming a sheet of white in front of us. Mom slowed down to a crawl on the interstate. We were only a few miles away from the cabin when Mom spotted a gas station and pulled in.

"I need gas and we need snacks," she said, handing me a couple of bills. "Go in and get whatever you want, okay?"

Bring back peanut butter Twix, you cowards!

Inside, the counter person—a retirement-aged man—was flipping through a magazine. He looked up when the doors opened, blowing in snow, and gave me a nod before going back to his magazine. I raided the shelves, and when it felt like I'd spent around forty dollars, I carried everything up to the counter. The cashier considered it—and then me—for a moment before he put down his magazine and stood up.

"Your parents know you're buying this crap," he said, not unkindly.

Encouraging it, jabroni!

"She's out there getting gas," I said. The man waved, and then went back to scanning the snacks about as slowly as anybody in the history of the world. "But I guess she didn't say I should get all of this."

The man smirked. "Well, you might get the vitamins you need."

There were a few odds and ends on his counter—a pickle in a bag, a few dusty-looking oranges, and a bag of almonds. I picked up the almonds and tossed them onto the pile.

"Protein," I said.

Protein, jackass!

"You all up here visiting?" the man asked, continuing to ring up the snacks. "We've got weather coming."

Most gas station cashiers barely registered my existence, let alone delivered a commentary about the weather, my residential status—the nutrient content of my purchase. And yet, Mitch here was taking a comprehensive inventory.

"You all should go for a hike down near the lake. It's beautiful this time of year. Violent, but beautiful."

Beep, the Twix. Five seconds and a comment about brunch spots. *Beep*, Pringles. Five more seconds, followed by a quick look into the monitor when a truck pulled up to get gas.

This guy.

When he finished ringing everything up and pulled out a few plastic bags, I was relieved—especially since he was practically bagging at light speed compared to his checkout abilities. Still, he talked as he worked.

"So you from the Cities?"

"Yeah. St. Paul."

"Oh yeah? I grew up in St. Paul. Can't say I miss it."

Just bagging groceries, bagging on St. Paul. This crotchedy-ass old dude sitting here like some kind of modern-day bridge troll, waiting to trouble anybody who decided they want to visit the North Shore.

I couldn't lie; I kind of respected it.

"Well, you must love living up here," I said, fully expecting him to look out the window at one of the most objectively beautiful places in the entire world and give me an uninterested shrug.

"You know what I love about up north? You can get away. You can get lost. It's not the same as the city, where yeah, I've been lost. Up here, getting lost still means something. You can lose a part of yourself if you're not careful—unless that's what you're trying to do."

He pulled the two bags off the counter and handed them to me. They were heavy, embarrassingly so for a gas station purchase. I let the bags hang at my sides, expecting the man to continue his story. Instead, he sat back down, picked up his magazine, and went back to reading.

"Well . . . goodbye?" I said.

It felt like there should be some sort of tearful or earnest endcap to his story. How he came up here to lose something, a burden that was now relieved. But all I got was a nod, a grunt, and a flipped magazine page.

When we pulled into the semicircle drive of the cabin, Mom and I looked at each other, surprised. The outside was trendy, the sort of place where your bohemian aunt might live. Chimes, a spiraling wind-catcher, and a bronze number plate highlighted the brightly painted yellow door.

"Well, look at this!" Mom said, putting the car into park. "Maybe we won't go back!"

The snow was really starting to pile up, which made me worry that the "weather" coming was actually a blizzard. But one quick look at the cabin settled me down because there was something about being snowed-in that was appealing. It was the middle ground between danger and freedom—you couldn't go out, but the snow wasn't a threat. Instead, you just resigned yourself to the fire, the hot chocolate, all the shows you hadn't yet watched. How many times had we done that as a family? Whether by conscious choice or the fact that a foot of white stuff dropped on us overnight?

Mom opened the door to the cabin and turned on the light.

"Oh shit," I said, unable to stop myself from laughing.

Cozy getaway my ass.

The room looked like the stunt double of the pictures on the rental app. Everything was in the right spot, was the right shape and color, but all of it was otherwise off. The sofa was beyond worn, and as soon as I sat on it a puff of dust emerged from the cushions like a ghost. The springs moaned, threatening to rip through the decades-old foam. Mom's "bedroom" was wedged into a corner between the fridge and the dining room table. If we tried, we could probably hold hands and touch the walls.

"This . . ." Mom pulled out her phone, checked the pictures, and then returned to staring in disbelief at the cabin. "This is . . . the place. Well, dang."

I was about to search out some silver linings—lemons into lemonade and all that—when I noticed something was spectacularly missing.

"Mom. Please tell me there's a bathroom."

Mom pulled out her phone and started scrolling. The more she scrolled, the less confident she seemed. She took one look around, as if maybe we simply hadn't seen the bathroom, and shook her head. I opened the door and walked outside. Despite the cabin's best attempt, the northern part of Minnesota remains unspoiled—the undefeated, heavyweight champ. I stopped and looked up. There were more stars here, which couldn't actually be true but when you stared at the sky, couldn't be denied, either. There wasn't a city light for miles and the snow lit up the area like a lantern.

I took a few steps around the left side of the cabin, all while remarking at the power of photography angles. This place was even tinier outside. A box, nothing more, with a single pipe chimney reaching from the roof. At one time it was certainly nothing more than a hunting cabin or an ice fishing stop-off at best. But with some paint and imagination . . .

A cozy getaway!

On the left side was an old canoe, resting on sawhorses, and a feeding trough so rusted out that it almost seemed intentional—Americana chic. Behind it was a small path that presumably led to the lake. I could hear it crashing in the distance. The reason they were able to rent this place at all, I'm sure. When I got to the far side, I found exactly what I was hoping I wouldn't see.

A shitbox.

Inside, Mom was trying to start a fire in the woodstove. She had directions open on her phone, which made me laugh at how completely out of our depth were.

"Outhouse confirmed," I said.

Mom nodded, poking a lighter into the stove to ignite the knots of newspaper she'd put at the top of the stack of wood. At first, I didn't think the flash of fire from the newspaper was going to last long enough to work, but the smaller pieces of wood below it slowly began to burn, followed by the larger wood.

"Well, at least we won't freeze," she said, standing up and dusting off her knees. She looked around the cabin and shrugged. "I mean, it could be worse."

"Mom. How could it be worse?"

Mom thought about it for a second and then snapped her

fingers. "There could be no 'house' around the toilet. Just a toilet in the woods."

"Your optimism annoys me."

"It's my superpower, honey."

Mom got busy unpacking the food and drinks we bought while I dropped back onto the groaning sofa, hoping to stare at my phone for the next hour, two. But I didn't have coverage.

"Mom, does your phone work?"

She checked her phone, cocking her head to the side as she lifted it up to the ceiling.

"It was . . . ," she said, moving closer and closer to the fire. "Ah! I have two bars here!"

I dropped onto the floor and scooted closer to the woodstove, which was already putting out enough heat to warm our house back home, let alone the cabin. I had one bar, enough to send Bri and Max a text detailing the villa's brighter spots, and to see that I had a single text from Leg.

My pulse quickened as I opened the message.

Hey, lady j. The non-skating, unbetrothed. Okay i will stop. so prom. i was serious

Every single one of my fingers turned into a thumb, all of them pointing in opposite directions. But for some reason, being out of town made it easier for me to say yes. Somehow the anxiety of what people—Max and Bri—might think had slipped away, buried under the falling snow. But how could I say it in a way that would make him realize that it was a real yes—that I shouldn't have made him wait?

You say yes, Juliana. That's it. Just, yes.

I typed out a quick "Yes," hit Send, and immediately put my phone away.

"What's that about?" Mom asked. She had her lawyer eyes on, and I tried to look annoyed. Innocent. "What? You look like somebody asked you to steal the Constitution."

She chuckled at her own movie reference.

"That's all this night needs," I said. "A Nic Cage appearance."

"Well, you are in luck," Mom said, dramatically pulling out a collection of VHS movies that she'd found on a shelf next to the woodstove. There was a combo VHS-television unit, which must have been high technology in its day. "We've got *National Treasure, Rocky IV, Fright Night, Bridges of Madison County*, and *Top Gun*."

"*Top Gun*," I said, and Mom said something utterly disturbing about shirtless men and volleyball.

For the second time in a week, I was watching *Top Gun*, which I would call "unexpected." This time, however, it was with Mom, leaning into our shared ability to riff on the different parts that Dad mocked or mimicked, sometimes inexplicably, even though he supposedly hated the movie.

"When the guy Slider flexes during volleyball," Mom said. "Do you know how many times he would do that when he took his shirt off to go take a shower?"

"Mom. Please."

"Oh, that's tame. I'm saying he was a nut," she said, laughing. "Like, who remembers that scene? And then goes around trying to make it happen?"

He's an animal!

Dad once told me you could learn a lot about a person based on their favorite scenes from movies. And not just regular movies, but classics—cult or otherwise. So, if you met somebody who loved *Star Wars*, their favorite scene shouldn't—couldn't—be the moment when Luke blew up the Death Star. Because that's too obvious. It was written to be everybody's favorite scene!

Woo-hoo!

Instead, your favorite scene should be anything else, anything that only you would notice. Something that would only make you laugh or cry. The thing that you and your sister quoted to each other right before you got off the phone. It could literally be anything, but it would tell you what you needed to know about how that person saw the world—what they'd been through.

We finished the movie and Mom convinced me to sit and watch *Fright Night*, a movie she'd watched with Dad when they were dating, and I said yes because what else would you do when you're staying in a creepy-ass cabin in the middle of the dark northern woods? But we weren't twenty minutes in before she was snoring next to me. It was another ten minutes before I stood, carefully, so as not to wake her, and turned off the movie.

I was immediately bored.

I checked out the board game shelf—nothing. I grabbed a deck of cards but there wasn't a table to play solitaire and the status of the carpeted floor was off-putting, to say the least. Eventually I put on Mom's long, extra-warm jacket and walked outside, planning on taking a few laps around the house—just to shock myself into a place where I could come back inside, jump under a blanket, and fall asleep.

It was cold outside, but not freezing. The snow was coming down harder, but after the rather warm spell of the last few weeks, it wasn't sticking—not that the fat flakes weren't trying their best. Once I was out there, I wasn't exactly sure I wanted to stay. I could use the bathroom and save myself from the indignity of stumbling into the late-night cold, running to and from the outhouse like a horror story.

Instead, I walked to the back of the house—to the path, which was just visible enough in the falling snow to give my bad idea credibility. The lake! At midnight! In the snow!

Let's go!

The first few steps were more treacherous than I anticipated, and I almost fell due to the sudden drop. But once I was underneath the trees, there was barely any snow and the path stretched before me like a ray of light all the way down to the rocky shore of Lake Superior.

Without experiencing Lake Superior—and that's the right word, *experience*—it was difficult to explain her sheer power, majesty, and beauty. If you were dropped on certain parts of her shores, you would think it was a sea. From the treacherous waves to the sheer size, Lake Superior made you pause.

Even from the path I could hear the waves crashing against the shore. It had an almost magical, kid-like effect on me—making me want to charge the beaches, ripping off clothing until I hit the water and dove in. To be clear: there was never a time of year when Lake Superior wasn't freeze-your-ass-off cold, but that didn't stop anyone. People even surfed the large winter waves, emerging with frozen beards and cemented reputations.

When I got to the beach, the only thing I considered taking off was my shoes and socks, just to feel the sand for a moment. But knowing I would have to walk up the path once again—and knowing the grating of sand in your socks—I decided against it and walked toward the loud darkness of the shoreline.

You could walk all night when it was like this, save the cold, and never second-guess your footing. A few feet offshore, there was an outcropping of rocks, slick with water, that, on a warmer day, would call my name, water temperature be damned. But on a cold night, it was the sort of thing that started and ended a story on the shores of Lake Superior.

Instead, I sat against a long-dried log, the evidence of generations of campfires tucked inside the windproof barrier it created. You could imagine people gathering around it—sitting on top, in front of it. A destination point, surely.

These were the sort of places Dad seemed to find instinctively. Whenever you'd ask, he'd wave it away or say something about his childhood. But he was unable to stay in one place, to ignore the next path he saw. Mom once said that she was the first thing he didn't leave behind. The way she said it was positive, but it still scared me. That one day, he wouldn't be there—would move on.

You should know better, Juliana.

But he did. Not in that way, of course. And his funeral told a different story.

The sheer amount of people who showed up was astounding. People from parts of his life that hadn't been lived in decades. High school friends. College roommates. People who knew him when he got the money from that aunt and gave surfing a try. Bought himself a ticket to Hawaii, only to learn that he couldn't get off his stomach—never even caught a single wave, as they told it. But there were four men who had obviously shared that same dream, who showed up and told me stories about camping on the beach, grilling fish and drinking beers and listening to him tell stories about a girl back in Minnesota.

When they pointed at Mom, it was like she'd somehow caught lightning in a bottle with Dad. If you heard him talk about her—about me—it was as if he was the luckiest person ever. Not a shred of regret, even when he was the only one who would go out and shovel snow or cut the grass.

It was too cold to be crying and the tears stung my cheeks.

I just missed him. And sometimes it felt like I wasn't allowed those feelings anymore. It was a knife in my side every time somebody looked at me as if I was somehow not okay for not being okay. As if their certainty that everything would be fine, or should be fine, didn't pierce my heart, making me wonder why I hadn't forgotten him as easily as everybody wanted me to.

Those people are candy-assed jabronis, Juliana.

I slipped into sleep effortlessly, despite the cold and the sand and wind in my hair. Perhaps it was Mom's jacket, impossibly warm and unfortunately long for almost any other circumstance. Like a sleeping bag with sleeves, Dad had said, and immediately regretted when Mom swatted at him. Or maybe it was the rhythm of the waves, crashing against the shore again and again, reaching for the sand only feet in front of me. Pushing and pulling, pushing and pulling, until my eyes closed. Until I was lost in a dream of years before.

A voice, calling out.

I love you, Juliana. I love you.

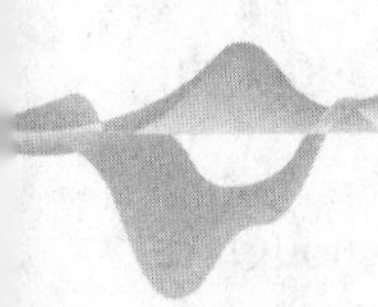

CHAPTER SEVENTEEN

I woke up shivering.

The sun was just rising on the far reaches of the lake. I was stuck to the spot, wedged between sand and log. My nose was numb with the cold, my back locked by the contortions needed to keep myself warm inside Mom's jacket. I couldn't move at first. It took a few breaths, a few attempts, before I finally pushed myself off the sand—like diving into cold water.

All the warmth I had created by going fetal dissipated as soon as I stood up. I couldn't get up the path back to the cabin fast enough. When I burst through the front door, I worried that I would wake Mom up. But she was already on the couch, bleary-eyed and holding a cup of coffee. I dove for the woodstove and tried to steal all its heat.

"Did you have a good walk?"

"Walk?" I asked.

"I assumed you went down to the lake when I woke up and you weren't here. It must've been cold."

I probably shouldn't tell Mom I accidentally spent the

night in a hollowed-out log on the shores of Lake Superior. While it was a mild night by Minnesota standards, it wasn't the sort of anxiety I wanted to introduce to her life. Was my daughter growing up normal? Was she on drugs? Does she randomly fall asleep in the wilderness?

I grunted because it was cold and that felt like enough to grant plausible deniability, if needed.

"What do you want to do today?" she asked, looking at her phone. "We have a very short window where it won't be snowing one thousand feet."

"Whatever you want to do," I said, my teeth slowly beginning to stop chattering. "Maybe we could get some breakfast downtown?"

"That sounds perfect. And then we'll go shopping."

I looked at her suspiciously and she shook her fist in the air.

"That's right, SCOTT. You hear that? I'm about to become a materialist again!"

Mom took her time finishing her coffee, maybe because she saw me thawing slowly. When I finally shed her jacket and we started getting ready, we jockeyed in front of the only mirror in the whole place, a modest amenity about the size of a dinner plate and held up by a piece of wire that had seen better days. Leaving the cabin was a test in either self-confidence or self-delusion because I was pretty sure neither of us looked fit for civilization.

"I don't even care," Mom said. "Who am I trying to impress?"

"Not Scott," I said carefully. Mom scoffed, pulling at her ponytail, as if to make it even more unruly, and then muttered something under her breath.

"The one time I need you to be a surly teenager and you totally let me down," she said.

"Me? What?"

"You should've put up a fight. Like, 'He'll never be my dad!' and that sort of thing."

Scott, that candy-ass.

"I believe my feelings were made known on this," I said, but then I couldn't tell if she was being sarcastic, especially when she realized that, maybe, she might have hurt my feelings. When she went to apologize, I stopped her.

"I just want you to be happy, Mom."

I could've told her that a puppy had died, that's how her face dropped. She looked past me, to the small window above the door.

"I mean, I can start now if you want—I hope that guy gets hit by a bus."

"Julie . . ."

Yes, one of those extra-large, accordion jobs.

"I don't know, Mom. It's just . . . he was never going to take Dad's place. Nobody will, ever. That doesn't mean it won't be nice for you to have somebody, or even for me to have somebody in that sort of, uh, role."

"I really thought I was . . . I don't know. Better?"

"Dad's like a virus that never leaves," I said. "Long-Dad. He just keeps affecting us."

"God, you don't even know how much he would love that analogy. Seriously."

I reached over and hugged her. When I let go, she didn't. She squeezed tighter and I realized this wasn't as much about Scott as Dad. Almost immediately, I had to stop myself from offering the same crooked logic everybody else suggested to me. I thought she was over Dad, or at least ready to take a step forward. But now, I'm not so sure.

"We could go to that breakfast place Dad liked," I said. "The one right on the water."

Mom nodded and asked if I'd drive. I grabbed my phone and the keys, and we headed to the car. When we got to the restaurant, it was nearly empty, and we sat right near the windows—watching Lake Superior crash into the shore and crawl back out into itself. My phone was dead so I charged it at an outlet next to the table. We sat there silently, waiting for our food to arrive, until my phone came alive—a flash of sound and light. I quickly muted the messages and alerts now that we were back in some form of civilization. Most of them were half-hearted reprimands about missing class, which reminded Mom she hadn't called me in sick. There were a few missed assignment alerts, too, which I would handle later. One text from Bri, a selfie of her and Max kissing and then another one of them laughing.

Young love, how disgusting.

And finally, a message from Leg.

Bet. We should probably go on a date or two or three first. For science

Message sent . . . yesterday. Great. He probably thought he was being really clever—sweet, thoughtful—and here I was some ungrateful hag who couldn't even open a text within a respectful amount of time.

You might be overacting, Juliana. That jabroni is ass over kettle for you, dear.

I fired back a text.

Only if it's for science

"You okay?" Mom asked, smirking. "You look like you just got asked to prom or something."

"What? Why would you say that? Were you on my phone?"

Subtle, Juliana.

"Well . . . wow. I was kidding," Mom said slowly. "But prom? That's . . . wonderful. Are you going to say yes?"

An intense heat started at the bottom of my neck and slowly spread to my face. I was wide-eyed, unable to move or speak or do anything except feel the extreme horror of having this conversation. And I didn't even know why. If anything, Mom and I had shared too much in our lives together. But for some reason this felt like an exposed nerve. Something I wanted to uncover slowly. At my own pace.

"His name is Leg," I said.

"Leg?"

Mom tried her best, but she couldn't stop herself from laughing. At first I was offended. He couldn't help it if his name was Leg! Or Francis! Jesus, Mom, and here I thought you were all social justice, queen of the underrepresented and marginalized. Power to the people and all that. But the outrage burned off fast. And I laughed, too. Because his name was Leg. And we were going to prom.

"His name is actually Francis," I said.

Mom thought for a moment. "Yeah, Leg is better. So how did you meet?"

I explained to her about *Top Gun* prom, an idea that made her almost spit out her orange juice. I told her about the meeting, the courting gifts—having me write my number on his skateboard.

"You're excited about this. About him," she said. "I can tell."

My first instinct was sarcasm, deflection. Nothing to see here. But I knew it was fraudulent straightaway. So, I gave myself a moment to acknowledge that I was excited. And maybe I hadn't been truly excited for something in a long time.

"I am," I said.

The waitress started unloading plates—way too much food—on the table and for a few minutes, the conversation was lost to biscuits and gravy and Mom asking if they had any fresh fruit. When we had everything, Mom popped a piece of cantaloupe into her mouth and said, "Okay, well, tell me about Leg."

It felt strange for his name to come out of Mom's mouth.

"He skates," I said. "His best friend is some guy named God."

Mom shook her head and said, "I'm not asking any questions."

"And I don't know. He's funny? And nice? And he wants to, like, letter in prom. Which isn't a thing, by the way. But he's been three years, and this is, like, his crowning achievement."

"Prom. His crowning achievement."

He's a candy-ass, my dear. And that's okay.

"I thought it was a bit at first—okay, it's kind of a bit," I explained. "But then I got to know him, and he asked me again and . . . I don't know. I like him."

"Does Max like him?" Mom asked.

"Maybe more than Bri would like," I said, laughing.

"Not a fan of Leg?"

"More like not a fan of *Top Gun* prom."

Mom shook her head. "Life is going to be hard for Max."

Took one too many bumps, that kid.

"So does that mean we need to go dress shopping?" Mom had never been the sort of parent who tried to influence what I wore, never made comments when I went through my wrestling T-shirt phase, or my flannel and ripped jeans moment—which was popular at the time, thank you very much.

You looked ready to rumble, Juliana. Bring it back!

But she seemed excited, even if she was trying not to let it show. Hedging her bets that I would want to go in full military dress or something.

"Yes. But I don't need anything expensive," I said.

Mom played it cool, nodding and smiling. Pulling up her phone and checking the situation on local shops, writing herself some notes. And so, there we were—me and Mom, happy about prom. My phone dinged and both Mom and I looked at it, sitting on the table. Even from here we could both see who sent it.

"Well? Aren't you going to read it?" Mom asked, almost giddy. I picked up the phone, swiped left on the message from Leg.

Just tell me when

Ben Franklin's was a kind of catchall department store, the sort of place that was second only to, say, Disney World in my childhood imagination. Dad would give me a five-dollar bill and let me run wild, buying anything and everything I could get my hands on. Most of it didn't make it home from the vacation—it wasn't exactly high quality—with the rare exception of a bracelet with my name on it. Not my full name, of course—despite Dad's grumbling, they didn't have it in stock.

"Maybe they finally have 'Juliana' bracelets," I said, pulling Mom into the store.

"Lord. Your father."

Inside, it looked the same as it did when I was a kid. Smaller, perhaps. But the shelves were still packed with the sort of surprises and mysteries that could capture the heart of any ten-year-old. I picked up a charm bracelet, then a miniature statue of the famous *Edmund Fitzgerald* ship that wrecked before Mom and Dad were born. It still sat on the lake's floor, supposedly, five hundred-some feet deep. I found

Mom standing at the front of the store checking her email.

"Didn't find anything?"

"No," I said, choosing not to say what I was really feeling: this place just didn't have anything for me anymore. "It was fun seeing it again, though."

Mom stared at me for a minute and then said, "Well, are you ready to 'Say yes to the dress'?"

"What? Now?"

Mom did a little dance that was more than a little embarrassing. "What else are we going to do? Go back and hang out in the cabin?"

"*Cozy getaway*, show some respect," I said, and she laughed.

What is a cabin, if not a cozy getaway in training?

Mom took my hand and we walked along the streets of Grand Marais, pausing to look in different shops and even going into one where I tried on a rather poofy dress and Mom ended up buying a nice, expensive bracelet for herself. Slowly, the shops became less dress-focused, and more other-things-focused. She bought a purse, and I found a bulky and warm sweater, then a painting of an unintentionally psychotic-looking loon for my room. At the final shop, a vintage clothing store called Sugar Britches, we found a pair of vintage Doc Martens and Mom forced me to try them on. Once they were on my feet, I couldn't deny that they made me look pretty badass.

Shit kickers for those who want to kick shit!

"Okay, these are amazing," I said, turning my foot to

model them for Mom, who pulled out her credit card and handed it to the store owner without a second thought.

"I really don't need a dress—at least, not today," I said.

"Wait—a dress?" the owner said. She was in her late thirties, dyed pink hair, an arm full of tattoos, wearing a chiffon skirt and a T-shirt for a band I didn't recognize. "What kind of dress?"

"Prom," Mom said.

"To go with those boots?" the woman asked. She clapped her hands and ran to the back of the store. She came back with a garment bag, laying it gently across the counter. "This came in as a part of an estate sale and I've been waiting for the right person."

I went back to the dressing room and slowly unzipped the bag, catching a whiff of mothballs and something else—perfume, maybe? At first, I wasn't impressed. The dress was old—vintage in the way the cabin was a cozy getaway. Nothing more than a swath of green polyester. But when I held it up, the dress shook out and I caught my breath. It was a classic swing dress, complete with a plaid scarf and a matching strip of plaid stitched into one of the pleats on the dress. I slipped into it like a second skin, tied the scarf around my neck, and stepped out of the dressing room.

Mom gasped. And then she started crying.

We got back to the cabin with a few more bags than I expected and a new appreciation for the idea of "retail therapy" because once I had those boots on my feet and the fabric of the dress against my skin, it was like the dam broke.

"That was fun," Mom said, arranging the bags on the small kitchen table. She started flipping through a collection of CDs on the shelf. "And you looked cute, Julie."

All I could do was agree with her—I'd felt cute.

I was also totally exhausted. And as much as the cabin kind of sucked, the bed and couch were definitely better than the cold ground, the effects of which were creeping up my body—calling me to sleep.

"Oh!" Mom said, pulling out a CD from the stack. "Oh God. Your father. He loved this woman."

Mom showed me the copy of an album with a tie-dyed buffalo on it. I'd never seen it before in my life.

"Now, if he were here, he'd want you to think that we named you Juliana after his great-aunt something-or-another that he'd one hundred percent never met in his entire life," Mom said, slipping the CD into the player. "But your father had a crush on Juliana Hatfield—so bad—and he just . . . he refused to acknowledge it. Like, what do I care? She's attractive. He's never going to meet her. Just own it, my guy!"

I chuckled as the music starts playing, aggressive indie rock with a singer who just sounded cute.

"Are you trying to tell me I am named after a nineties' indie music crush?" I said.

Mom looked down at the floor, smiling. "That's one of a few things your father and I left unresolved," she said. "But when I agreed, you'd never seen a happier person in your whole life. And I swear to God if he could see you in those Docs right now, he'd pull me aside and say something about his plan coming together."

"What plan?" I asked.

"That you would be happy, Julie. Happy, healthy in every possible way, and totally, uniquely you."

I fell asleep to the music, letting it take me to a time when Mom and Dad were younger. Him playing Juliana Hatfield in the car and her playing it cool, not only because she liked the music but because she liked Dad more than some stupid crush. There he was, bleached hair and ill-fitting T-shirt, holding Mom close as they listened to the music. I had to wonder if he knew then that he would want a daughter named Juliana, if he had an equally nineties pop culture boy's name—Evan, Kurt, something. And even though I knew I was dreaming and that everything I was seeing about my parents was nothing more than my own creation, a mash-up of old pictures and stories and perhaps the eggs I ate for breakfast, I didn't want it to end.

I woke up and it was cold. Like, really cold. Mom was standing next to the woodstove, poking at its innards. The CD was no longer playing. When I shifted on the couch, she noticed and said, "Well, it seems like you're not supposed to burn all of your wood at the same time. So, we have a decision to make, kid. Go buy more wood or go home early."

I didn't have to think about it. I stood up, grabbed

my bag, and started stuffing. Mom chuckled and started packing her stuff as well. It took us less than ten minutes to get everything in the car. As Mom locked the front door, she called me over.

"Let's take a picture. Never forget, all that."

She held her phone out in front of her, framing us shoulder to shoulder and smile to smile. When she snapped the picture, it was just us and the bright yellow door behind us. A normal vacation, nothing at all wrong with the cabin. Just a happy family. Happy enough that you might not even have questioned the absence of Dad.

And just like that, we were back on the road. At the first stoplight, next to the gas station, I looked over and saw Mitch slowly bagging some snacks for the next round of people who had traveled north looking to remember or forget something.

Get that protein, you candy-ass!

As we waited for the light to change, I texted Leg.

Tomorrow?

It took him seconds to reply.

You're on the calendar, J

I smiled and Mom missed the light changing because she was smiling at me, not goofy but genuine. Behind us a car honked—maybe the only thing that could've made her look away.

CHAPTER EIGHTEEN

The next afternoon,I tore through my closet. I had no idea where we were going or what I should wear, so I pulled out a pair of jeans and a T-shirt, with a cardigan and my new Docs. I looked in the mirror and thought. Yeah, I'd be happy if I was Leg.

He better be! Unless he wants me to whoop that candy-ass!

We agreed to meet at six p.m., which was still thirty minutes from now, so I sat on the couch and mindlessly turned on the television. A replay of last night's Adrenaline was on and it might as well have been a sedative, because suddenly I was slouched on the couch—not even stressed about Leg or what was, essentially, my first-ever date, save for a couple of group "dates" to the roller rink in middle school. I wasn't about to focus on that or give Mom a reason to reach the same realization. Until the doorbell rang and my entire stomach shot into my throat.

"I'll get it!" Mom sang, nearly leaping down the stairs in excitement. I watched her open the door.

"You must be Leg," she said, turning to mouth *He's cute!* to me from behind the door.

"Uh, yes, ma'am. You can call me, uh, Francis if you'd like."

"Would you like that?"

"No, ma'am, not at all. Leg is fine."

I couldn't help myself, I laughed. Leg stepped through the door, looked up toward me, and then immediately shielded his eyes.

"Is that last night's Adrenaline? I still haven't seen it!"

I scrambled for the remote, turned it off, and apologized. Mom shook her head.

"Oh great. Another one."

Leg didn't have a car but offered to ride double on his skateboard, which sounded cute though dangerous, so I went back inside and grabbed the truck keys. When we were sitting in the cab of the truck, it felt somehow smaller than it should. I looked at him and asked, "So what's the plan?"

Leg shifted nervously. "You're eighteen, right?"

"Are you taking me to a strip club?"

"What? No. Why would you think that?"

"Just checking off the list of places you need to be eighteen to enter," I said.

"Uh, no, I was thinking we could go play mini golf. At that place by the light rail line."

Give him hell, Juliana.

"Can Can Wonderland? Why didn't you just say so?"

Leg risked a small smile. "Oh, you're messing with me, aren't you?"

"I am, in fact, messing with you, Leg."

"My mom told me not to be myself," he said. "I think she really meant 'Don't try to be funny.' She does not think I am funny."

"This is a trend, isn't it?"

Leg leaned back in his seat. "Genius is never understood in its own time. I tell God that all the time."

"And what does God say?"

"'But idiocy is.' Or something. I can't remember. I have healthy self-esteem and don't need external affirmations."

Can Can Wonderland was a sort of bar-restaurant-mini-golf-art-space almost at the St. Paul city limits. As we got closer, Leg seemed to relax and began to just talk normally, not constantly try to impress me or crack a joke. I was not as comfortable. It was strange to have another person in the truck with me—not that I never rode in it with Dad. But since he'd been gone, it had just been me. And Leg took up a lot of space, a lot of air, especially when he was talking. It wasn't bad, just different.

"You okay?" he asked.

"Yeah, just getting mentally prepared for the whuppin' I'm about to put on that candy-ass."

Leg stopped dead and stared at me. "That impression of the Masked Man is the most beautiful thing I've ever heard."

It better be, you jabroni.

"So you're a fan?"

Leg scoffed. "I'm more of a disciple, Julie. A hard-livin', smack-talkin', jabroni-kicking . . ."

"Man of the people!"

We both called out the last part, hands to the side of our mouths just like the Man. The sort of thing that sent electric shocks throughout arenas across the world. If I hadn't already liked Leg, there was nothing holding me back me now. It wasn't that I needed to be with somebody who liked wrestling. If anything, the dating pool in wrestling circles was . . . small. And tragic. And filled with all manner of mouth breathers and life-size replica championship belt wearers. I wanted somebody I didn't have to explain the fascination to—somebody who didn't want an apology for loving it.

This kid may be a candy-ass but he's got good taste . . . for a candy-ass.

"So . . . I assume you saw last week's Adrenaline," Leg said.

"Leg, I cannot properly express my excitement to you."

"I had this whole plan to get a ticket. But then I was, like, how will it look if suddenly I am on television in the front row. By myself. On prom night."

"Uh. Awesome?" I said.

"You are obviously more confident than I am."

"I don't think we can go to prom now," I said flatly.

Leg did a double take and then rolled his eyes. Then he got weirdly nervous and said, "It was before I had a date, okay? And I was going to rent us one of those, like, ridiculous

Hummer limousines and maybe even rent out all of Memory Lanes. You know, next-level prom shit. But maybe I'll just go by myself."

I turned and looked out the window, mostly so I could smile without him seeing me.

"I don't need—or want—all that," I said. "Just so you know. But Max and I are going to watch it after prom. Maybe you could come over, too. You're buying the pizza, though."

"It seems only fair," he said.

Leg smiled as I turned into the parking lot for Can Can, which was packed. We had to circle a few minutes before I could finally pull into a spot. When we got out of the truck, Leg reached over and grabbed my hand—a bottle rocket launched inside my stomach. And he did it so casually, so coolly, that I didn't even hesitate or wonder if it meant more than it did. I just let him hold my hand, letting go only to open and hold the door for me. And then it was me who reached for him, as we walked into the busy space. He looked just as surprised, just as happy as me.

Leg was not good at mini golf, even by casual noncompetitive standards. He had already chased five errant shots across three holes, apologizing as he retrieved his ball from a hole halfway down the course. Meanwhile, I was having the game of a lifetime. Three holes, three holes in one.

"I'm going to talk to the manager," Leg said. "I'm pretty sure my club is crooked."

"I probably should've told you I'm essentially a pro," I said.

And though I was obviously joking, I was kind of not joking at the same time. Dad was self-proclaimed "good at everything," besides bowling it seemed, which was less of a boast and more of a legitimate fact. At least, when "everything" could be sectioned off into Ping-Pong, carnival games, any game that garnered tickets and therefore prizes, and, yes, mini golf. "If only those were skills that made one wealthy," Mom would say, and Dad would feign offense, anger even, and then begin quoting Marxists and Leninists, which led Mom to turn on her attorney brain and always ended up with them either laughing or essentially making out.

I didn't want to think about making out.

Lip-smackin' . . .

"Why are you so red?" Leg asked. "I'm the one running my ass around this course like it's a five k."

Shoulder-rubbin' . . .

Don't think about making out. Don't think about making out.

Good old-fashioned making out!

"Nothing," I said, almost defensively. My voice too high, the words too fast. And suddenly I couldn't stop myself from saying more. All of it horrendous and deeply embarrassing. "I was thinking about something and then trying not to think of something and, well, I just need to stop talking but I can't. So. Yeah."

Leg leaned on his putter like an old-timey cane, totally

amused. And maybe he figured it out, I don't know, but he graciously changed the subject. "You're feeling intimated by my skills, aren't you? It's only natural, Julie."

This jabroni right here.

"Your skills. Leg, Leg, Leg. You have no skills."

"I will bet you literally anything that I will score better than you on the next hole. Anything."

"You have nothing I want," I said. "And besides, I've heard it's bad form to crush the spirit of your date. So I'm trying hard not to do that, but you're just very bad at this. Leg, help a girl out."

He closed his eyes, opened them, and took a step closer to me.

"If I beat you on this hole, I get a kiss."

The big size-fifteen boot is about to go up this jabroni's ass!

I was immediately frozen, unable to move or speak or do anything except nod because I wasn't totally opposed to the idea. And, yeah, I was factoring in how I was going to win because I'm just built that way, cute skater kid or not. Kiss or not.

"I shoot first," I said. "Put the pressure on you."

"Be my guest," Leg said, bowing. I scooted past him, trying to focus on the hole. The hole, the Squirrel Scrambler, was one of the easier ones—and one that required more luck than skill. You just had to hit it into the right chute and it would deliver you a hole in one. Leg hadn't hit a straight shot all night. The trick was to focus on accuracy instead of power.

"You look like you're about to play in the Masters," Leg said. "And I'm trying not to be insulted, honestly."

I shrugged and bent down to line up my putt.

Give it to him, Juliana!

When I stood up, I tried to clear everything from my mind. To center myself. I thought about the sports greats who have come before me—Jordan, Serena, The Rock—the ones who stood in the annals of time, legends who did legendary things. They might even make a T-shirt about this.

I took a breath. Blinked once. And sent the ball toward the chute.

"Get in the hole!" I yelled, which shocked and embarrassed me and amused Leg, especially when a couple of college students started laughing at me. But something bad was happening. I don't know if it was my aim, my touch, or perhaps my brashness, but the ball was already traveling too far to the left. When it hit the side of the wooden ramp and bounced nearly back to the tee, Leg chuckled.

"Try to keep it on the course while I go get my two," I said, looking over my shoulder at him.

"Don't miss. Again!"

"I could miss three more times and I'd still be safe!"

I sunk the two putt and flexed on Leg. The college kids laughed again. I didn't even care because this kid wasn't hitting this putt. Not tonight. Not ever.

This jabroni doesn't have it, Juliana. Your virtue will be safe!

Leg licked his thumb, put in the air like he was checking

the wind. He rolled his neck, stretched his arms, and then did a couple of weird almost-lunges before he put his ball down and then, without any aligning, aiming, nothing, just hit it like some kind of toddler who was happy to be there.

"GET IN THE HOLE!" he yelled, obviously mocking me, which made the college kids laugh even harder—clapping, everything. But I couldn't worry about whether they were laughing with us or at us because this damn kid. This damn ball.

"Holy shit," I said.

"HOLY SHIT," Leg said as the ball traveled down the chute and dropped into the hole.

He was still on the tee, hands over his head—putter clutched above him like he was searching for a lightning strike—jumping up and down with pure joy.

It's a sad day in Mudville, Juliana.

He ran and grabbed me in a huge hug. I expected him to kiss me, too, but he didn't, just put me down—eyes wide, mouth gaping—and said, "I don't want to overstate this, but that might be the best thing that ever happened to me."

It was impossible to be annoyed with him or about losing the bet, because he was just . . . giddy. Even though I trashed him completely on the next fourteen holes—and it wasn't even close—it didn't matter. He was like a little kid.

Give his candy-ass a trophy.

And I loved it. I loved the way he kept talking about it. The way he called God, who was skating and could obviously care less, and told him about it. He was so damn consumed with the hole in one, I was pretty sure he forgot about our bet. Which was, honestly, for the best. I had no idea how to kiss another person, the mechanics of it all, let alone doing it in public with everybody watching.

Millions and millions of fans, here for one reason!

When we turned in our clubs and were out in the parking lot, he was still raving—asked a couple who were about to go in if they'd ever heard such a story. They laughed, probably thinking he was high, and proceeded to take a wide berth around us. At the truck, Leg went to his side and jumped in, still talking.

This kid has the game of a toddler, Juliana.

I got in and started the truck. As it idled and the heater kicked in, I sighed once—trying to get his attention, maybe. I didn't even know.

"So . . . ," I said. "What now?"

I wasn't sure if he was some kind of evil genius mastermind or just flying by the seat of his pants.

Let's just say I know the answer to this one, Juliana.

"Well, we could go see God and them. They're over at the Lair. Or we could—"

I didn't know what came over me. Maybe it was residual aggro from all my peacocking during mini golf. Or maybe it was getting tired of waiting for him to do it. Or maybe I just wanted to kiss him and didn't want to wait any longer.

So I kissed him.

And he kissed me back.

Then a couple of people walking past hooted and hollered

and I pulled away. We sat there in a sort of shocked silence; the only sounds were the muffled crowd noise from inside Can Can. A car passing on the road behind us. A mountain of silence building between us, one that needed to be punctured so it wouldn't become too awkward to climb.

"That was the luckiest damn shot of all time," I said.

CHAPTER NINETEEN

The next morning I woke up earlier than Mom because I wanted to make sure I'd gotten all the bubbles out of my stomach, all the nerves settled, any evidence that I had my first kiss last night wiped completely from my face, my body, my entire being.

None of it worked. Mom took one look at me and immediately said, "So you had fun last night?" I couldn't help but scream at her, high-pitched and frazzled. A confession without words. All she did was laugh and give me a hug, which I resisted until she said, "I'm happy for you, Julie. That's all. Okay?" She kissed my hair and then went about getting her coffee. But she was humming a little too much, a bounce in her step that was a little too obvious.

On Monday I studied myself in the mirror, searching for any glimpse of *happiness* or *joy* or *I kissed that skater kid* on my face before Max showed up with Bri to drive to school. When Max honked and I walked outside, I must've looked like a total goblin because they were both like, "What is going on?" And I said, "Nothing!" Trying to be chipper but also completely worried that, somehow, I was going to betray myself. I got in the back of Max's car and pulled up my hoodie, hoping nobody asked me another question again ever.

This is all very mature, Juliana. Let no one tell you otherwise!

"So, my mom is really excited about the idea of us going to prom in a limousine," Bri said. "Which I realize is kind of extra but she's a bit unstoppable at this point. I guess what I'm trying to say is that we're taking a limo to prom."

"I cannot wait to stand on the seats and stick my head out of the sunroof," Max said. "A couple bottles of sparkling wine in my hand. Pointing at all my boys as we pull up to prom."

"Your boys. Okay," Bri said.

"What? I'm down with the boys!"

"In the entire time we've been dating, I have never seen you with a single boy, let alone boys, plural. It's okay. You only hang out with girls. I think that is cute."

"For what it's worth, being 'cute' isn't the compliment you think it is."

"Who said I'm complimenting you?" Bri said, turning around in her seat to face me. "Care to weigh in here?"

When she saw my face, it was like she had super X-ray vision because she squinted at me and said, "What's up with you?"

"Nothing," I said.

Way. Too. Fast.

And now Max was looking in the rearview. They peppered

me with questions that I deflected like I was a black belt in karate, tossing each one to the side with a simple word or shake of the head. But I was afraid they'd get too close to the events of my date with Leg, the kiss, so I held up my hands.

"I'm going to prom with Leg," I said. "Jesus, Spanish Inquisition in here."

"Nobody expects the—" Max started but Bri stopped him.

"Not the time." She smiled big at me. "Well, now I'm glad we got the limo. You and Leg are obviously joining us."

She raised her eyebrows, as if hoping there was more I wanted to share—which I absolutely did not. I couldn't look at her anymore.

"I'm happy for you Julie," Max said. I caught his eyes in the rearview mirror and searched his face for any trace of irony, any coming joke. But there was nothing. I nodded. I didn't want to talk about Leg with him, not right now at least, and when we got to school, I tried to ditch them in the parking lot, a hint that Bri either didn't pick up or intentionally ignored because she was step for step with me to the doors, up the first flight of stairs—all the way to Wentz's class, even though she was supposed to be on the other side of the building.

"Okay, spill."

"I already told you. Me and Leg. Prom. Woo."

Wooooo!

"Yeahhhhh, I'm not an idiot. I can see it all over you."

Just then Leg came riding up on his skateboard, only to

get yelled at by Wentz, who threatened to toss the skateboard out the window. To which Leg said, "Wentz, why are you always trying to have beef with your top student?"

"You're not my top student, Leg."

"By a certain rubric, though, I could be."

Wentz was going to laugh, I could tell, but rather than show his hand he went back into his classroom. When Leg turned to me and Bri, he went strangely rigid—as if he didn't know how to hold his body or what to do with his hands, even though they were holding his skateboard.

"Oh. Uh. How are you? I mean, you cool? Uh, cool."

He patted me on the shoulder.

This jabroni.

Patted me on the shoulder! He dropped his skateboard to the ground and took off down the hallway, faster than he probably should. I wished I had such an escape because Bri had this all-knowing look on her face that I absolutely hated.

"Never mind," she said. "That's between you and . . . Leg."

The way she said his name bothered me and made my skin light on fire at the same time. I had to work to regulate my voice, not to go all shrieky-screaming-girl-in-love on Bri.

"What do you mean?"

You're out here trying to fake the master, Juliana!

"Nothing. Obviously, nothing happened that would take you and Leg to the next level. And you're totally not, like, just all happy and excited despite your best attempts to hide it. So, nothing. Don't worry about it. You're totally fine, nothing to see here."

"That's right," I said, walking into Wentz's class.

"Talk to you at lunch!" Bri said brightly, laughing as she disappeared down the hallway.

Leg met me at the door of the cafeteria, still awkward, but I couldn't stop myself from going all mushy inside when he handed me another orange soda.

This isn't going to be a thing. I demand Orange Julius!

"Thanks," I said, and no one word had ever been so hard to force out of my mouth so casually.

"No problem. All I had to do was skip third period. I'll do that anytime. For you."

I couldn't keep my composure. "Seriously?"

"Yeah, sorry. That was too much, wasn't it? I totally skip third period every day—you just give me some direction now. See that? You're a good influence, Julie."

This jabroni right here.

"So, um, are we going to sit down?" I asked.

It felt like every pair of eyes in the cafeteria were on us as we walked; every one of them could see inside me—could see how happy I was as Leg joked about pulling out a chair for me, even though they were attached to the table. I felt like a damn fool and was enjoying every minute of it.

When Max and Bri showed up, Max did a double take.

"What? Stop looking at me."

"Uh, okay . . ."

"Stop looking at her," Bri said. "You're being a creep."

"I literally just walked up to the table! I didn't know this was an eyes-down zone!"

"Ladies, amirite?" Leg said, offering up a fist bump to Max, who was now completely conflicted about what was happening and what he should do.

"Oh, please do continue this conversation. Julie and I will benefit from both of your knowledge of 'the ladies,' I'm sure," Bri said.

It was enough to break whatever—was it tension?—was surging through my body. I was simultaneously overloaded with anxiety and happiness, a potent mixture that made me capable of saying and doing some truly cringeworthy stuff. So I decided I wasn't going to say or do anything. Not a word or a movement until it passed, no matter how long it took, realistic or not. I lived here now.

"Anyway . . . ," Max said, trying to recalibrate a bit. "I'd like everybody to be prepared for the very real possibility that Julie and I might not be able to attend prom after tonight."

This got everybody's attention.

"What are you talking about?" Bri said. "Because I already bought my dress."

"Me, too," Leg said, and despite herself, Bri laughed.

Max stood up and started unbuttoning his shirt, which is something that immediately drew the attention of a group of guys two tables away. Their catcalls drew the attention of a few more tables, and soon we were in the middle of an event.

"What in the hell are you doing?" Bri whispered.

Max just smiled and continued unbuttoning his shirt, pausing on the last button with a smile until he opened the shirt and revealed a loud, vintage Breathtaking One T-shirt.

This guy.

"What is happening?" Bri said. "What does this have to do with prom?"

"Oh! The book thing at the Mall!" Leg said, nodding his head in appreciation.

Max looked pleased with himself, for the reveal—for the attention he was getting from what was now a majority of the cafeteria. He sat down as a few younger kids walked by and told him he was "built different."

"Thanks, guys—I know."

"You know," I said. "Lord."

"Annnnyyyyywayyyy," Max said. "Julie, had I known this was going to lead up to quite possibly the biggest wrestling event of our lives—the biggest event of our lives?—I don't know that I would've been as excited about a chance to go see a cut-rate self-help guru. But . . . I'm excited."

The last part was pure Max, behind all the jokes, and what little bluster he had was somebody who was intent on making this special—not only for me, but also for himself. For younger Max who, like me, could still see the shadows of the Breathtaking One in his prime. Would show up to a book event for that reason alone.

"It's going to be awesome. Maybe I'll try to get us kicked out. Really give him the business from the crowd. When's the last time the Breathtaking One had any heat?"

This made Max visibly nervous. "Yeah, well, you remember I work at the Mall, so . . ."

"I'm all about that wrestling life, Max."

He stared at me, trying to figure out how serious I was—and I wasn't sure myself. Yet.

We will give him the business, Juliana.

I don't know what I expected when we got to the Barnes & Noble at the Mall of America, but it wasn't a line stretching out of the store or a harried clerk who told us under no circumstance would the Breathtaking One (she called him Mr. Erwin) be able to take pictures or do anything other than sign his latest book. His gaze lingered on me and Max as he said this last part.

Move along, book jockey.

He paused for two more seconds before his joy-killing announcements took him down the line of the growing crowd. Max turned to me and said, "What's the chance that either of us are going to follow those instructions?"

"Slim to none," I said.

He paused, looking up and down the line, and then into the store. He did this a few more times before sighing heavily.

"And how interested are we in . . . getting the book that came with our tickets signed?"

That would be even slimmer to none, jabroni.

I stepped out of the line first, but Max wasn't far behind.

We walked slowly toward Orange Julius, both of us waving to Marvin, who looked like he could use somebody like me to show up on the regular and give him some company.

"I'm sure he would love that," Max deadpanned. "You want to grab something to eat?"

Orange Juliusssssss!

But instead, we ended up at a fancy cheeseburger place in the newer food court, which was empty—like everyone had split to go to the Breathtaking One's book signing. You could hear the music above us, the soft whine of a vacuum in a store somewhere in the Mall.

"This is a damn good burger—why don't I come up here more often?"

"Because Kathy packs you dinner," I said. Max snapped his fingers in recognition and took another bite. It was nice to have him here with me, not working. Usually when I wasn't at Orange Julius, the Mall was a lonely, solo endeavor. And for the most part, that was by design. It was a way of being alone without having to be alone. People walked by second by second and none of them would ever speak to you.

We sat there not talking for what seemed like an hour before Max said, "So, it's weird."

"You're going to have to expand."

"Like, we're graduating. And we have . . . significant others. Julie, we could have sex."

"Stop. Please."

"I'm just saying things are changing! Our bodies are changing!"

This was the exact moment when a woman and her two young daughters walked by, which made us both laugh but also collect our trash and start walking back toward the parking garage outside of Barnes & Noble. It was late; the Mall would be closing soon. Not that Max couldn't use his Orange Julius street cred to gain some after-hours access.

We walked slowly and I was enjoying the time and trying not to think about how things were legitimately changing. How in a few months we might be in different parts of the state—different parts of the country, depending on where we ended up going to college. If we even went to college! How many more opportunities would we have to simply walk around the Mall of America together?

Now I'm going to cry.

"This is fun," I said to Max. "I'm going to miss this."

Max stopped walking and stared at me. "Okay, you're not going all emo on me, are you?"

I punched him. As hard as I could. "I'm trying to say that I'm going to miss you—and all of this—when we graduate. Like you said, things are going to change, Max!"

Max rubbed his shoulder and conceded the point. "I mean, yes. Some things. Like, I'm not going to work at Orange Julius forever."

What!

"But some stuff is forever. Like me and you? That's not changing. Not for me."

"Maybe," I said.

"What? Julie, c'mon."

"Max, we don't know! You can't say that some stuff is forever. You literally can't tell me that, okay!"

Max stopped walking right outside the rotunda. The crowd for the Breathtaking One was gone. We were alone, and even Marvin had already turned off the lights and gone home, which meant he'd knocked off a little early.

"Seriously. This?" He pointed at me and then himself. "That's not in question. That's a forever thing for me."

I tried not to cry, but I couldn't stop myself. I stepped closer to him and he put his arms around me and let me cry into his shoulder.

"I miss him," I said. "Still."

"I know," he said.

"And I'm tired of feeling like everything is constantly in flux. It's just—" I stopped talking because I wasn't sure where I was going with that sentence. Or to be truthful, I'm not sure I wanted to stumble back into the fog of unknowing, of feeling like everything was up in the air—able to be changed at a second's notice.

"I mean, that's not bad," Max said. "Being in flux is also growing, I think."

I looked at the tile floors of the Mall, polished but plain. I could see a distorted picture of my face, the light above me like a halo.

"I wish we'd gotten to see the Breathtaking One," I said, looking at the doors of the Barnes & Noble, which was already dark inside. "It seems like the perfect end to everything."

"This isn't the end. C'mon." As he said this, Max turned to look at the dark store. He put an arm around my shoulders and squeezed. "Plus, he would've probably been a real asshole."

"Maybe."

"Or you would've freaked out and asked him, like, about the best match of his life."

"Well, that's dumb because it's the Mall match, obviously," I said.

"Uh, I hate to do this to you," Max said, stepping away from me as if I'd just said something he couldn't believe. "But that is not the best match."

"Maximillian, please. You're embarrassing yourself."

Max's eyes shot open and his mouth tried to work out something else to say. He finally shook his head and managed, "Mid-Atlantic. Nineteen ninety-three."

I had my response halfway out of my mouth when I stopped myself, because dammit.

"Yeah. Shit. Breathtaking One versus the Masked Man. Steel cage, loser leaves town."

"Oh, you mean the one where he totally cheated the Man out of his title shot because the Breathtaking One couldn't stand the fact that the Man might get a bigger pop?"

"You seem . . . angry."

"It's not anger, it's passion."

Yeah, jabroni!

A hint of a smile crossed Max's face. He shook his head and said, "Why don't I just admit I'm wrong and save us all the effort of this argument?"

I shook my head.

Suddenly it was like a time machine back to my living room, back to my father. To me and Max sitting on the carpeted floor, eating snacks and laughing at how angry Dad would get when the different angles played out in ridiculous ways. How he would snort at jokes and snort a different way at certain wrestlers he thought were nothing more than a gimmick in tights.

"Where do you think the Man actually is these days?" I asked. Max looked like he was ready to cry for some reason, and I didn't know if it was the fact that he was just caught up in the emotion, or if we, too, were in flux and couldn't stop anything from changing.

He paused. "Parts unknown, of course."

CHAPTER TWENTY

The next few weeks went by at light speed—a blur of finishing my extended essay, lunches mediating among Bri and Max and God and Leg. I even went skating with Leg and God, and Leg joined me and Max for a Friday night Adrenaline viewing. It had a strange feeling of normalcy, as if this had been the way people had always been living and I was just now figuring it out.

Wentz was impressed with my extended essay, especially my developing insights into kayfabe. When we didn't see the Breathtaking One, something switched inside me. On the one hand, it would've been exciting seeing him in person. On the other, he was in a Barnes & Noble. Signing books. Sitting there, just as shackled by his calendar as I am to school. That night, I went home and wrote the rest of my essay.

Should anything ever be preceded by the word *never*?

Yeah, *Never break kayfabe* had a certain romanticism to it. And it was a philosophy that could take you pretty far down the road of life—especially if you never had to question anything. But Mom and I did. We lost something indescribable and gigantic. A person who should've been with me for a long, long time. It was unfair and seemed random at times. But he was gone and that was real. And instead of trying to figure out whether it had been an angle or a work or anything else, maybe it's just okay to say that it sucks—so, so much—and that's reality, at least for right now.

In wrestling, the term *work* means any pre-scripted events. The best *works* have always been the ones that come with a grain of truth, a sliver of reality that makes you pause and think—*Wait, am I being worked here?* On the other side is a shoot, which is when a wrestler decides to break from the story. Works don't work without reality, and shoots don't work without kayfabe.

Maybe kayfabe was actually the thing that helped us see reality more clearly. Maybe it wasn't a choice between the two, but an acknowledgment they were inextricably combined. Just like happiness, and grief, and every part of life.

So, Never break kayfabe? Maybe, maybe not.

But either way, I still wanted to believe.

And so, when the week of prom came, I didn't even try to fight the butterflies, the excitement. Before then, prom had always been something that snuck up on me—oftentimes I wouldn't know it was even happening until the next day was flooded with social media pictures, stories about faceless people who did things that were so far out of context they seemed nothing more than fiction. And yet, now, I could feel the expectation that must have preceded every one of those pictures, every one of those stories.

On Saturday I woke up to excited texts from Max and Bri—promising to be at my house that afternoon, a limo in our driveway. I spent the rest of the day with Leg, eating brunch and him trying to teach me how to stay upright on a skateboard, which ended up with me falling on top of him in the grass.

Laughing. Kissing. Happy.

I got home a little sunburned and feeling frazzled by the extra hour I spent with Leg, only able to pull myself away when I started doing the math—trying to remember the last time I actually did my hair. Mom was waiting at the top of the steps. Holding three cups of Orange Julius in her hands.

"I thought we could get ready," she said. "All of us."

I took a cup and tried to freeze the coming tears with a sip. Not that it would matter around Mom. I just didn't want to start the night that way—I wanted to keep this, for lack of a better word, special.

Mom took a tentative sip of her own drink and cringed. "Okay, let's get you ready."

Mom was not exactly flashy with her makeup, hair, or clothing. But once she got me seated in front of the bathroom mirror, it was like some kind of inner cosmetology demon was unleashed. She had opinions. Lots of them.

"Not the side part, Juliana!"

Mom rested her hands on my shoulders and looked at me in the mirror. I could already tell she was fighting off tears, but she didn't let any break through. Instead, she picked up her Orange Julius and took another sip, followed by another cringe.

"I can't believe you like these things," she said. "Of all the aspects of your father's DNA to embrace."

Your mother has besmirched Orange Julius for the last time, Juliana!

I finished off my cup and tossed it into the trash can next to the toilet. The third one sat on the counter and, for a second, we both looked at it. I had no idea if it was me or Max who started the trend, but I couldn't think about all those extra cups right now.

"What time is Leg supposed to be here?" Mom asked, gently curling the last strand of my hair. She let it fall and once again looked at me in the mirror.

"Soon," I said, still thinking about Dad and Orange Julius. Trying not to mess up the bare minimum eye makeup Mom had helped me put on. Mom could see it, I guess, because she handed me a tissue. I dabbed the insides of my eyes and forced out a laugh. "Do you think Dad would've liked all this?"

Mom looked at me strangely. "What do you mean?"

"Like, getting me ready for prom. All of this weird stuff. Do you think he would've enjoyed it?"

Mom smiled big, the sort of smile I hadn't seen from her in a long time. As if it was being powered by something outside her body. She leaned down and wrapped her arms around me, saying, "He would've loved every single minute of it."

Every single one, you jabroni.

I was sitting on the couch in my amazing dress, waiting for Leg, and suddenly the whole situation seemed ludicrous. Like I was a debutante from the old movies my grandfather liked to watch. Sitting and waiting for a date, some clean-cut boy in a skinny tie, to show up and, golly shucks, take me out for a malt.

Or an Orange Julius.

When the doorbell rang, my entire body reacted. I stood up and Mom rushed down the stairs, holding out a hand for me to wait. To be presented, I guess. I didn't say anything because she looked so happy. She straightened her pants, her shirt—as if she was the one being picked up—and then opened the door.

When she gasped, I wasn't sure what to think. The following laughter—real, from the belly—was confusing enough that I rushed down the stairs to find Leg and God dressed like the two main characters from the original *Top Gun.* Flight suits complete with patches that said "Maverick" and "Goose." Aviator shades. God even had a fake mustache. I couldn't say it wasn't a surprise, but it also worked in a way that was hard to articulate in front of my mother.

"Wow," I said. "This is commitment."

"It's what I do," Leg said. He smiled and then hit God in

the shoulder. "Also, I told God he had to come for the effect. He was worried you'd think he might be, like, a third wheel."

I feel the need. . . .

"My date is . . ." He motioned to the limo, parked outside. A rather bored-looking girl with purple highlighted hair and a nose ring waved, then went back to checking her phone. Suddenly Max popped out of the roof holding a bottle of . . . something.

The need for speeeed.

"Are you ready to party, Julie?" Max raised the bottle in the air and took a big swig. He turned sheepish and quickly told Mom, "Don't worry, it's sparkling grape juice. . . ."

"Noted," Mom said, guiding me out the door by my shoulders. I assumed she wanted to take some pictures, so I turned and waited. Leg and God were already walking down the driveway, to the limo, laughing and pushing each other.

Mom raised her hands, made a pretend camera, and snapped a picture. She winked and pointed to her head. "Got it here. Go have fun."

When I got inside the limo, Bri scooted over so I could sit next to her. She gave me a hug and then a grimace.

"I blame you for this," she said, pointing to Leg and God, who'd obviously made an impact on Max. The more she watched them, though, the more her charade of anger crumbled. She finally sighed. "They do look cute. Especially Max."

I half expected Max to be wearing the same suit he'd

worn to every "dress up" function we'd ever attended together—a mock trial we did our sophomore year—always with the Pokémon tie that he'd had since we graduated fifth grade. But he was wearing a tuxedo, and I took a second to appreciate how good he looked. I didn't notice Leg staring at me at first and when I caught him, he played it off—quickly told God a story about some guy at the skate park that got both of them laughing.

Classic.

We drove the long way, along the Mississippi River, rolling down the windows despite the devastation to our hair. The constantly changing air of a Minnesota spring traveled through the limo like a song. Max stood up through the window again, only to have the limo driver yell at him loud enough that he apologized and sat down. The whole time Leg and I were exchanging looks, quick and nervous. At one point Max caught us and smiled. I wanted to reach across the seat and punch him.

A million ass whoopins for you, sir!

The smile wasn't mean or even amused. It was happy. The longer he looked at me, the more he smiled, and now I wanted to punch him for being such a cheesy idiot. We'd been through so much together. Not just losing Dad, but . . . everything. All the small things, good and bad, that make up a life together. Max was right—some stuff is forever.

Your tag-team partner for life, jabroni.

Thankfully the windows were open, because I wasn't about to start crying in a limo on the way to the prom. Just as we pulled up to the venue, Leg took a metal drink stirrer out of the empty minibar and hit it against Max's empty bottle of sparkling grape juice.

"I'd just like to say thanks to Bri for not killing us when we totally ruined her prom experience," Leg said, which got a hearty "hear hear" from God. Max squeezed her shoulders. Bri, for her part, took a benevolent bow. "And also, to Julie, who has officially allowed me to not only letter in prom—"

"Not a thing," I cut in.

"—but also, uh . . ."

Leg looked sheepish, perhaps for the first time since I'd known him. He looked at God, then to me, and then to the floor.

"I just want to say thanks to, uh, Julie, because she's the first person who ever, like, actually wanted to go to prom with me? I think?"

It made me blush, so I turned and looked out the window at all the other students laughing and walking toward the entrance of the RiverCentre. We weren't the only limo but people were still staring, as if waiting to see who would step outside. Perhaps Leg and God sensed this because they looked at each other, did this weird high-five thing, and scrambled out of the limousine before anybody else could even stand up.

Once we were all outside, it was evident that Leg and God were the only ones who'd taken *Top Gun* prom literally. There are a few aviator glasses here and there, which I'm sure people thought would be enough to get a laugh—to be praised for their creativity. But then they saw Leg and God, who looked like they could be extras in the film. The attention to detail, a little too good.

It makes those other kids look like a bunch of jabronis.

God and Leg led us into the prom like a royal procession. People were taking pictures, stopping for selfies—everybody laughing. When we got inside the venue, however, I was no longer looking at Leg and God.

The entire room was decorated to look like an air hanger, complete with different images projected onto the wall of airplanes taking off and landing. The tables were full of *Top Gun*–themed snacks and drinks. Even the teachers had gotten into it in different ways, dressed in various levels of costumes and commitments to the bit. For a moment both God and Leg looked surprised. They turned to Bri.

"What?" she said, trying to seem annoyed. "We had a budget. You all approved my decorations list. I couldn't let this suck."

Leg picked her up into a bear hug, which broke her façade and she laughed. Then he came back to me and led us all to the center of the room. I half expected for a spotlight to appear and Leg to lead a choregraphed dance, which naturally made me want to hide under the various tables that dotted the sides of the room. Instead, he gave me a kiss on the cheek and then ran to the stage and grabbed the microphone.

He tapped it twice, squinting into the crowd, and said, "Okay, welcome to *Top Gun* prom!"

"There isn't much else to say except—" God said, and

cued the DJ who put on "Danger Zone" by Kenny Loggins. I was pretty sure most of the crowd had no idea what this song was or how it connected to *Top Gun*, but the energy level had eclipsed any sort of logic or reason. The dance floor immediately came alive with people yelling and dancing. Leg hopped off the stage and walked straight for me, a single arm held out.

He stopped before he took my hand. God gave him a look and then, as if they'd rehearsed it a hundred times, they both pulled off their flight suits with one rip of Velcro. I was ready to shield my eyes—ready to run out of the prom and just cut my losses because, nah. But suddenly Leg was wearing a tuxedo.

"I'm only half committed to the bit," he said, taking my hand and leading me out to the dance floor.

Okay, now that was smooth, Juliana.

We danced. We ate. We laughed. The whole night seemed to spin by in a maze of lights, minute after minute of an experience that felt both new and yet familiar. Something we'd all been promised in any number of movies, television shows, and nostalgic stories from adults. However, unlike most things that fell into this category, the prom seemed to be holding its own—to be holding up.

When Leg and God tried to "make break dancing happen," I tapped out to go sit at a table. Bri followed me, both of us sipping our drinks as we watched our dates dance with God.

"I am really sweaty," Bri said, squirming and adjusting her dress. "Like, to the point that I think I just want to go home and not wear this dress anymore."

"Max will be excited," I said, and she nearly spit out her drink.

"Yeah, I mean replacing it with, like, basketball shorts and a T-shirt."

"Unfortunately, that probably won't change his level of excitement."

"Fair," she said. "You aren't staying in your dress when we go home to watch your old wrestling guys, are you?"

"You can't call them old wrestling guys," I said, and Bri shrugged. "But, as far as I know, it's sweatpants for me. But Jesus, I'm not counting anything out at this point. The flight suit to tux reveal? Inspired."

"I hate to admit it, but those idiots pulled it off."

Max, Leg, and God all ran up to us, sweaty and slapping high fives.

"Hey, it's almost time for the limo to get us, right?" Max asked. Bri pulled out her phone and said, "Yep."

"Can't be late," Leg said, smiling.

Bri blinked. "Late? For the television?"

Leg and Max looked at each other and started laughing.

"Just tell him we're ready, okay?" Max said.

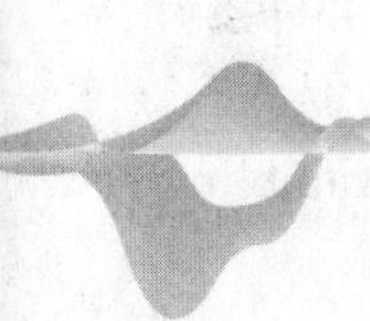

CHAPTER TWENTY-ONE

None of the boys told me or Bri where we were headed or why they kept laughing like a pack of idiotic hyenas. When we turned toward the Mall of America, I sat up in my seat. The lights, the signage for Adrenaline were like spotlights in the darkest night.

"I texted Marvin. He's going to let us in the employees entrance," Max said, and I basically tackled him in a bear hug and refused to let go until he said he couldn't breathe. Even then, I didn't want to. "Hey, this was Leg's genius idea."

"Let's see if it works before you go throwing around credit," Leg said.

I didn't immediately attack Leg and I wasn't exactly sure why. He looked thankful, too.

"This night needed some big hairy dudes slamming into one another, in a totally and completely heterosexual way."

Bri looked utterly confused, perhaps even horrified when she realized what was happening. "Are you serious? We're actually going to the event? But Julie's mom is expecting us at their house!"

Top Gun *prom, leveling up!*

"Trust me," Max said. "Julie's mom will understand."

I put my arm around Bri and said, "You're not going to know what hit you."

"Yeah! It might be a metal chair!" Leg said, scrambling out of the limo with whoop.

"Metal chair? What?!"

Climbing out of the limo, reality hit me in the form of three security guards, burly and blocking the doors to the Mall's entrance. Inside, I could see the lights—could hear the chanting, the feet stomping.

"Gentlemen," Max said, giving them his best salute.

"Wrestling? That's for kids!" Leg said, before Max grabbed him and pulled him away from the door—down the sidewalk. Barely out of the guards' view, Max stopped at a nondescript green metal door. He gave two quick knocks and a few seconds later, it opened with a metallic groan.

"It's about time," Marvin said. He was still wearing his Orange Julius hat and apron.

"Did you bring them?" Max asked, and the man sighed, hesitated, then held up a brown paper bag.

"If I get fired, you're going to be supporting me in the lifestyle to which I have become accustomed," the man said, holding the bag back when Max tried to grab it from him. "Right?"

"Yeah, yeah. I'll keep you in weed and comic books, Marvin."

Marvin, you old jabroni you.

When he took off his Orange Julius hat, a long gray ponytail appeared, which he smoothed as he inexplicably handed me the hat.

"I'll want this one back," he said. "I just now got it worked in the way I like it."

"Okay?"

"You'll get your hat back, Marvin, now can I have the bag please?" Max said.

Marvin studied Max one last time before handing over the bag. And then he excused himself, cutting through our group. Outside, he immediately lit a joint and started walking down the sidewalk.

"Okay," Bri said. "So, just to recap: we're sneaking into the Mall of America with the help of a pothead and a secret entrance."

Max reached into the paper bag and pulled out four Orange Julius hats and aprons. But Bri shook her head and refused to take the outfit from him until he said more.

"This was Leg's idea—these are our disguises. We can stand on the counter and watch the show."

This time I didn't stop myself from attacking Leg. I grabbed him and kissed him despite being crammed into a tight hallway with some of the best friends anybody could ever hope to find.

"Thank you," I said.

Leg, obviously flustered, just nodded and took the Orange Julius hats from Max, passing them out. I pulled Marvin's hat over my unruly hair. Max handed out the aprons. There was no way this would work because who was going to really believe that we were here to work at Orange Julius wearing prom dresses and tuxedos. But even if we only got to the end of the hallway, it would be worth it. The hope was worth it, even for a few moments.

I find great hope in a flying elbow off the top rope, Juliana.

Max looked around the group, straightening Bri's brim. When everything was to his liking he said, "Okay, this passage will drop us in the middle of the amusement park. My guess is there will be no security guards inside the park, so we should be able to walk to the back entrance of Orange Julius and . . ."

He held up a ring of keys, jingling them in the quiet hallway.

"My boyfriend the third key holder," Bri said.

"With great responsibility . . . ," God said.

" . . . comes a degenerate like Max who wants to take us to free wrestling," Leg finished. The word "degenerate" seemed to briefly shake Max's resolve. He didn't like texting his friends in class and now he was sneaking those same friends into the bowels of the Mall of America to defraud a national sports media company, all with the help of an aging pothead.

It's okay Max, nobody likes a guy without flaws. They call those people candy-asses.

"It's going to be fine," I said. "I still think you're a good person."

Max seemed to steel himself to the idea of dereliction.

"Okay, well, let's do this," he said, leading us down the hallway, which was long and dark and went on forever before we finally heard the low roar of the crowd, the stomping of feet, and the entrance music of a wrestler who just recently joined the company, Josh "The Horror" Stifter. When we came to the door, Max took a deep breath. Then he pushed it open, and we spilled into the empty amusement park.

The roller coasters and other rides loomed above us like sleeping giants. With every step, the noise of the crowd—the sheer energy of a live wrestling show—grew. And when we got to the Orange Julius back door, which opened with a simple turn of Max's key, I couldn't believe it was going to work.

But it did. Two minutes later, we were sitting on the counter of the Orange Julius. Two different times, security guards walked past and didn't give us a second look.

"The power of Orange Julius," Leg said in my ear. If he only knew. It felt fitting, honestly, to be sitting on that counter. To wait for the next walk-out with the same anticipation I had when I was a kid.

After The Horror pinned Jax the Giant, the lights went down and the walk-out music for The Legend blared, shaking the foundations of the Mall itself.

And there he was, standing in the middle of the ring, microphone in hand.

"It looks like this place is in serious need of a little . . ."

We all screamed the response—"HEART!"

It is astounding how beautifully simplistic wrestling fans are, Juliana.

The Legend looked around the room, waiting for the din to quiet down before he started speaking again. But before he could say anything, Stixx's music lit up the crowd and suddenly that jabroni was running down the aisle, sliding headfirst into the ring and jumping up as the crowd collectively had the first ever group stroke. Before he even said a word, the next theme music popped off and me and Max looked at each other, almost not believing our ears.

Oh God, not this candy-assed jabroni.

The Breathtaking One spun around—arms wide—at the mouth of the tunnel. He was wearing one of his traditional, highly ornate robes—they supposedly cost him six figures, or so the rumor went. Being that breathtaking took intent and money, which was something the slobbering masses would never understand. If you believed the Breathtaking One.

He strolled down the walkway, stopping to take a selfie with an older fan who seemed to be more than happy to surrender his phone. When he finally made it to the ring, one of his "attendants"—a scantily clad young woman—they never aged, it seemed—sat on the ropes so the Breathtaking One could slip through with little effort.

Juliana . . .

The Breathtaking One moved to the center of the ring where, for a moment, the three wrestlers allowed themselves to break character, to share with the crowd a singular moment of disbelief that they were in the ring together. I could feel Max's eyes on me, but I didn't want to look away. Too many times, people told me that wrestling was pointless or tried to make me feel embarrassed or shameful for loving something. But right then, in a room full of thousands of other believers, I knew it was all true. Maybe not kayfabe, but a bigger truth. And somehow it was better.

Juliana . . .

The Breathtaking One was the first to speak, raising the microphone to his lips and saying, "Well, well, well . . ."

People, again, lost their shit. And in all honesty, it didn't matter what any of them said. They could simply stand there for the next hour and it would be enough.

It's almost time. . . .

Stixx held up his hand. "Thirty years ago, on this same stage, one of you stood here for 'Stand Tall at the Mall.' The other was still shittin' his pants."

The crowd laughed, booed, every single emotion they could muster. He swiped his hand to the side, trying to silence the crowd, but the only person who could do that at this point was The Legend.

I want you to know something. . . .

"But if you remember . . . there was one more person in this ring that night."

The crowd exploded.

Our conversation has been one of my great joys, Juliana.

It hit me in the gut and I could start bawling right there on the counter. Not that anybody would notice, because everybody knew who the other giant was. Before his music hit, before he took that first step onto the walkway, I stood up on the counter so I could see him.

But it's time, jabroni. Okay?

Okay.

And the Masked Man walked out of parts unknown and took his place in the ring.

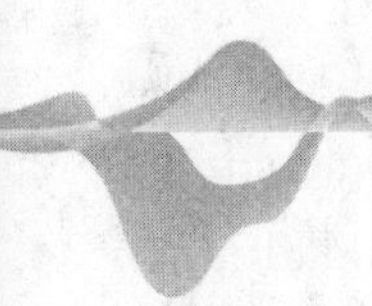

CHAPTER TWENTY-TWO

It was electric.

We stayed late, enough that between prom and the professional wrestling I felt like somebody had tossed my body from the top rope a few hundred times the next morning. I picked up my phone and every message was from Leg.

We killed prom

Bri would agree

Bri loves me

Top gun forever

I was probably still grinning when I got to the kitchen, because Mom raised her eyebrows but didn't say anything. She sipped her coffee and smiled behind the mug.

"Did you all have fun?"

"Yes. It was . . . amazing."

This made Mom put her coffee down and stare at me. Maybe it was because I couldn't stop smiling or because I couldn't remember the last time I had said something was *amazing* with that sort of tone, but that was exactly what it had been—*amazing*.

"And Leg?"

"A total gentleman," I said, trying not to blush. After the limo dropped us off at my house, we walked around the neighborhood, looking up at the stars, trying to extend the night as long as we could. It was horribly PG. Holding hands. A kiss or two. The sort of thing that I would almost be embarrassed to give somebody the play-by-play of the next day because, well, there weren't many actual plays. But the whole thing felt right. For the first time in a long time.

"I think we're going out again this afternoon," I said. "With Bri and Max."

Mom sniffled. "Why am I crying? You're happy, right? You look so happy. Jesus, why am I crying?"

I sat down at the table next to her. Something had changed and she could tell. I couldn't say that it was good, not entirely, but something—someone—had been released. It wasn't good or bad, just different. Quieter, maybe. New.

"I am happy," I said.

I drove my truck over to where Leg and God were skateboarding and watched them for an hour before Leg tossed his board in the back of the truck, hopped into the passenger seat, and gave me a kiss. Once he was buckled in, we headed to Bri's house. She had the door open before I could knock and, to her credit, didn't give a sideways glance to Leg—just a hug for both of us.

"We're already upstairs," she said, and we followed her up the winding steps.

When Max saw me, he gave me a nod—so casual, so grown-up. He was flipping channels on the television. Leg dropped next to him and Bri on the other side. I sat between Leg's feet and leaned against the couch, watching the channels flip by until Max finally landed on a movie that I'd never seen before.

And for a moment, it felt like this was how it was supposed to end.

No. Not end.

This is how we move forward.